Lord of Night

ERICA RIDLEY

Chapter 1

London, 1817

Miss Dahlia Grenville hunched in the shadowed entryway of the St. Giles School for Girls. Her once-pristine white silk gloves were marred with splinters from the well-worn broom in her hands. Ash from this evening's hearth made their fineness almost undetectable.

The old abbey that housed the boarding school had also once been very fine. Long before centuries of foot-falls had warped its marble staircase dangerously uneven, before decades of vagabonds and ruffians had managed to crack every pane of the colored glass windows, before the neighborhood surrounding the walls had become home to gaming dens and workhouses and indigent children who had seen far more of London's underbelly than any person ever should, the abbey had once been a symbol of hope. A sanctuary from the secular world. A place of love and peace.

Dahlia's goal was to bring back that lost security, even in those dark rookeries. To once again make these walls a shelter from the past and a bridge to a better future. She couldn't guarantee her girls heaven.

But she'd die trying to give them a better life here on Earth.

Unfortunately, being the second daughter to high-born parents had not exactly prepared Dahlia for becoming a headmistress. An outside observer might opine that her parents hadn't prepared her for anything at all, apart from making her come-out curtsey as a debutante and reasonably acquitting herself on the dance floor at Almack's.

None of that mattered. Dahlia ignored the cramping muscles in her back and shoulders and forced herself to keep sweeping today's accumulation of soot and dirt back out onto the street. Although it was no glamorous task, it allowed her to end each day with an accomplishment. Make her girls' world a little cleaner. Sweep the darkness back outside where it belonged.

Yet she knew they needed more. A lot more.

Her dowry, while not inconsequential, was not of the caliber to attract fortune hunters. More importantly, those funds went to the husband, not the bride—should that unhappy day ever occur. Which meant pursuing this dream had required her to call in every favor she could, beg every charity-minded soul from Bond Street to Grosvenor Square for donation after donation, until at last she'd secured enough funds to open her school.

To *open* it. Not to keep it running.

The plan to fill the six habitable bedchambers with one worthy young lady apiece had flown right out the drafty windows. Not one but *four* desperate girls now filled nearly every tiny room, each of the now twenty-three children more grateful than the last.

Some came from the streets. Orphaned, abandoned, homeless. Others had run away from dark places that could never be homes. Brothels. Workhouses. Drunken stepfathers.

Dahlia had promised them all a better future. Was *determined* never to send a single girl back to the horror they'd narrowly escaped.

These children were counting on her with their lives.

But there was rent to pay. Clothes to purchases. Mouths to feed. Dahlia had just finished serving the evening stew, and all she could think about was where to find tomorrow's. There was enough bread for breakfast, and even a hunk of cheese left over for lunch, but when the bell tolled the supper hour once again...

A scream rent the dank air, cutting through the smog-filled streets with piercing desperation before being just as hair-raisingly muffled by some unseen source.

Not again.

Broom in hand, Dahlia flew out of the entryway and onto the dark street.

Even a neighborhood as poor as theirs was supposed to have a night watchman, armed with a bright lantern and a sturdy cane. The only light came from the sliver of moon overhead, and the orange flicker of tallow rushlights in the windows of residents with enough money to afford a few candles.

She glanced to her left, toward the intersection of seven well-trafficked streets, where a large pillar rose up from the darkness toward the moon. By day, its six sundials told the time from every angle. Tonight, not even a watchman dared call the hour, as was his duty.

St. Giles was on its own.

A tell-tale rustle jerked Dahlia's gaze to the right, just in time to see two kicking feet dragged about the corner and into an alley. Fury billowed through her veins. She gave chase before it was too late.

"Help! *Fire!*" she yelled as her boots smacked against the foul cobblestone.

There was little chance the villain intended to set any fires, but yelling *Despoiler of young girls!* was unlikely to garner aid. From bawdy-house madams to fashionable courtesans, a fair portion of London's economy thrived on the exploitation of sexual favors… and a disinclination to meddle into others' business.

On the other hand, every resident in the St. Giles rookery lived in mortal fear of fire. No matter how much or little its residents possessed, an unchecked fire could burn entire blocks to cinders.

A few windows opened overhead as she rounded the corner into the alley. Dahlia didn't slow. In some neighborhoods, the mere presence of witnesses could stop a crime. Not this one.

No one would be coming to help. If Dahlia wished to save the young girl flailing in the arms of her assailant, she would have to do the rescuing herself.

"Stop!" she commanded in the booming voice she used as headmistress.

Startled, the ruffian paused to glance her way. The brim of his scuffed hat cast all but his scarred chin into shadow.

"Step away from my daughter at once," she demanded in the same implacable tones. "The watchman is on his way."

The ruffian hesitated, although it was hard to say whether it was due to the implicit threat of gaol or the mystifying improbability of four-and-twenty-year-old Dahlia giving birth to what she could now see was a six-teen- or seventeen-year-old girl.

"Ain't no watchmen in the rookery. Not tonight." The ruffian spit into the alley with contempt. "Come any closer, and I'll treat myself to both of you."

"You shall not." Rather than step closer, Dahlia lifted her heavy broom and swung at the villain's head with all her might.

There was no chance of the impact causing him any permanent harm, but the surprise of the attack and the noxious cloud of dirt and soot that exploded in his face were enough to cause him to release his grip on the girl's wrists.

With a frightened sob, the child leapt away from her attacker and toward the relative safety of Dahlia's side.

As much as Dahlia would have liked to envelop the terrified girl in her arms for a reassuring embrace, there was no time to spare. The blow from the broom had dislodged the villain's hat from his head, but it hadn't knocked him out.

Fists drawn, he launched himself away from the brick wall and toward the two young ladies.

The broom clattered to the broken cobblestones as Dahlia grabbed the girl's hand and hauled her out of the alley and back onto the main street. The abbey was less than a block away. If they could just make it to the front door—

Horse hooves clopped up from the direction of Seven Dials so swiftly that Dahlia nearly stepped into the path of the rider in her haste to get the terrified girl away from the ruffian in the alley.

They weren't going to make it. The villain's footsteps were right behind them. Both directions were blocked.

With the moon at his back, the man on the horse was bathed in darkness, his face obscured from view. From his perch atop his black steed, the man seemed impossibly tall and improbably strong. He was probably lost, and would be on his way soon. The biggest miracle was that he'd paused at all.

The ruffian's feet pulled up short a careful distance behind them. Dahlia's shoulders tensed. The moment the gentleman rode away, the girl's attacker would punish them both.

"Help," she gasped, knowing it was useless. Everyone knew that the wisest path through any rookery was as fast as one's horse could run. "There's a man trying to hurt us. He tried to…violate…"

Before she could get the rest of the explanation out of her mouth, the rider had already turned his horse's nose toward the alley. "Do you have somewhere safe to go?"

"The St. Giles School for Girls," she answered automatically. "But the man—"

"I'll take care of him. You get to safety." He eased the horse off the street and into the alley. "I'll be back."

Sure he would. Dahlia's teeth clenched. He didn't even know what he was looking for.

"Big hands, scarred chin, lost his hat in the struggle—" Dahlia shouted after the rider, but it was too late.

The gentleman was already racing down the alley in search of a ruffian who no doubt would never be found. Nor would the rider. A few blocks away, the good samaritan would tire of the fruitless search. He'd push the scared countenances of two unfortunate young ladies from his mind, and settle down before a cozy fire in his safe, warm home several miles from here, never to return.

Dahlia took a deep breath. This was exactly why her school was so important. Everyone deserved someone they could count on. Especially children with nowhere else to go.

"Thank you. For everything." The girl lowered her head, shoulders shaking.

Dahlia retrieved her fallen broom and scooped up the ruffian's hat. Knowing it would not be here when he returned to fetch it was a hollow, petty victory, but sometimes that was the only victory one could have.

She turned to the girl. "What is your name?"

"Molly," the child stammered.

Dahlia nodded. "Shall I walk you home?"

Molly lowered her gaze. "I sleep behind the bakery. Ain't all bad. The bricks behind the oven stay warm well into the night. Needn't worry about me."

"I know I shan't worry about you." Dahlia sighed. She was about to make a terrible financial decision…which was the only way she could face herself in the looking-glass. "Because you're coming with me. I am Miss Grenville, headmistress of the St. Giles School for Girls. You are our newest student."

"I'm…what?" Molly's eyes narrowed. "How do I know you ain't a madam?"

"I cannot prove it," Dahlia admitted. "I can only be honest. If you'd like to come with me, you are welcome to. If you would rather not, that is also your prerogative. I shan't chase you down either way."

Molly frowned in hesitation. "A madam woulda promised she weren't a madam."

"Your choice." Dahlia brushed off her dress. "Come or stay. What will it be?"

Molly's face brightened and she lowered her eyes. "I never been a student before."

"Then come along," Dahlia said briskly, herding the girl away from the alley and toward the street. "We're both out after dusk, which you can see is not a wise choice at all. From this day forward, I expect you to be in the dining room for supper, face and hands washed, at precisely eight o'clock every evening, along with the rest of the students."

"I... That is... I..." Molly stared at Dahlia speechlessly. Her face flushed. "Don't have any money."

"The St. Giles School for Girls does not require its students' money." Dahlia smiled as warmly as she could to hide the fiscal disaster of having yet another mouth to feed. "Don't worry. You are not in any debt. We do require a strong work ethic, adherence to the house rules, and strict attendance at every meal and every lecture. Are these terms acceptable?"

"I... I... *Yes!*" Unshed tears glistened in Molly's eyes. "I'd *love* to be a student at your school. I can be the best student your school ever seen."

"I wouldn't expect anything less," Dahlia agreed

without the slightest surprise. Mostly because every other student at the school had joined under similarly desperate circumstances and had instantly made heart-breakingly similar promises of obedience in all things in exchange for a morsel of food and a place to sleep. "Come along, then. I'll introduce you to the others."

"Thank you," Molly said quietly. "Thought I was about to have the worst night of my life. Mighta turned out to be the best."

Dahlia fervently hoped her boarding school would indeed be the answer to many prayers. Two dozen girls with nowhere else to go were counting on Dahlia to keep them safe. She swallowed the lump of worry in her throat. Tomorrow, she would come up with a plan.

No matter what, she had to find a way to keep the school afloat.

Chapter 2

Inspector Simon Spaulding raced his horse through the crumbling alleyways in search of the villain who had assaulted the two ladies.

Surely his Bow Street companions would shake their heads if they could see him now. Simon worked at least days a week, taking the shift through the night, and *this* was how he chose to spend his off-duty hours?

But Simon had never been interested in helping *some* people. He was committed to serving and protecting *all* people. Especially the young lady who had begged for his help, even though the bleakness in her eyes that indicated she had learned never to expect anyone's help at all.

That was the sort of person who needed it most. The sort who was most unfairly preyed upon by people like...what had she called after him? *Big hands, scarred chin, lost his hat in the struggle.*

Simon smiled despite the circumstances. That was the sort of information one investigator might provide another to aid in a case. Not the sort of details one would expect a young girl to note in the midst of a struggle, nor to have the presence of mind to convey to a Runner before he gave chase.

Especially since Simon hadn't even mentioned his occupation. There hadn't been time to do more than—

"Halt!" he shouted as he glimpsed a large man trying to sneak into the crevice between two buildings.

"Ain't done nothing!" When the man turned to snarl up at Simon, moonlight fell upon a gnarled scar on his chin. He wore no hat, and kept his burly hands curled into fists at his sides.

Simon pulled his horse alongside. "A pair of young ladies a few hundred yards back beg to differ."

"Then they're liars. Can't prove anything."

"What about the marks on her?" Simon asked coldly. Neither woman had mentioned any marks, but there were bound to be bruises in any struggle.

"Marks on her?" the man repeated in disbelief. "What about the marks on *me?* The older one came at me with a broom. Bloody near knocked out half of my teeth!"

"Then you admit it." Simon reached for his iron handcuffs. "Come with me. You are fortunate it was a broom to the head, and not a brick."

"*She's* the lucky one. If you hadn't stuck your nose in our business, I'd a—"

"You'd have done what, exactly?" The ice in Simon's voice more than sharp enough to kill.

Rather than answer, the man turned and sprinted toward the next alley.

Simon leapt from his horse and gave chase, tackling the man into the closest brick wall. "My name is Mr. Spaulding. I am an investigator at Bow Street. You are coming with me."

"Bloody hell," the man muttered.

Simon secured his wrists in iron shackles, then walked him back to Simon's horse, where a pouch contained a rope for leading criminals to the closest watchtower.

The watchtower, however, was empty. The night watchman was nowhere in sight.

With a sigh, Simon headed back toward the Magistrates' Court.

Luckily for the handcuffed man swearing under his breath as he stumbled beside the horse, Bow Street was less than a mile from where they'd begun.

Too bad. Anyone who accosted a woman deserved far worse than an uncomfortable twenty-minute walk.

When they arrived at Bow Street, the daytime inspectors had long since gone home to their wives or to the closest alehouse. Simon locked the malefactor in a cell with a tin of water, and sat down to write up his notes for the first officer to arrive in the morning.

He liked being thorough. Performing his duties the

way they were supposed to be done was what he did best. Some might say, it was the *only* thing Simon did.

When they called him "lone wolf," he took no offense. They were right. He was wed not to his job, but to this city.

Idle and disorderly, Simon wrote at the top of the paper. It was a catch-all crime that encompassed everything from prostitution to public drunkenness. Although its punishment didn't come close to atoning for the innumerable assaults this villain had likely perpetrated on countless young women over the years, the law could only prosecute what it could prove.

At the very least, this man had not gone free. A month in prison may not cause him to mend his ways, but it would keep him off the streets for now. Small consolation, perhaps, to the women who would have liked to see him rot in gaol forever.

Simon frowned and put down his pen. No one should believe their city had forgotten them. Not the young or the women or the poor or anyone at all. Everyone shared the basic human right to feel safe.

Starting with having an active night watchman on duty. Simon made another note to look into the missing guard, although it wasn't much of a mystery. Even though recent reforms meant that watchmen were now paid, in the poorer areas of town this often meant a coin was passed to some elderly gentleman to mind the post while the watchman on duty spent the rest of his pay on Blue Ruin.

Anger skated along Simon's skin. Everything about that situation infuriated. Leaving innocents unprotected. Shirking duties. Cheating the system. Visiting the public house instead of attending to one's responsibilities.

He would see to it that the watchman on duty was immediately sacked, and an alternate appointed. There would be no second chances. Simon had no pity for a man who left his post.

Just like he had no pity for the would-be debaucher rattling the iron bars of his cell. The rules applied to everyone. The world was black and white. Simon stayed on the good side and did his part to rid London of the bad.

After finishing the last of his paperwork, he locked the main door and remounted his horse. He could have hired a hack. He could even afford a carriage.

He preferred to ride a horse.

Ever since he'd joined the force, Simon's habit was to take a different path to and from work each day. If he had taken the direct route home, he would not have been present to interrupt tonight's attempted assault.

He had no doubt that the ruffian would still have run away from the intrepid young lady who had corked him with a broom.

Simon smiled at the image. He couldn't imagine what anybody would be doing with a broom in the midst of a moonlit rookery—he doubted the St. Giles streets were often swept even in the daytime—but the young woman who had wielded her impromptu weapon had been courageous indeed.

Since he had promised to return, he would stop by quickly. If everyone at the school appeared to be asleep, he would continue on without awakening them.

Everyone at the school was not asleep.

The headmistress from the alley answered the door on the first knock.

"Good evening," Simon said, his pulse quickening. Just when he'd thought he had concluded the last of the day's mysteries, here was another. Standing right before him.

The slender fingers holding the candle were encased in gloves of extraordinarily fine silk, which would normally be so much of an anomaly that one could be forgiven for thinking the wearer wasn't from a rookery at all.

These particular gloves, however, were stained at the tips and frayed at the edges. Making them more, rather than less, of a mystery. They were not the sort of gloves one purchased for manual labor, and yet clearly they had been used for just that task. Anyone who could not afford silk gloves would never allow the sole pair in their possession to be treated so badly.

The gown the headmistress was clothed in was exactly that—a *gown*—rather than the sort of dress one might expect the inhabitants of a rookery to possess.

Like the gloves, the gown fit beautifully and was treated shabbily. Hems were noticeably torn and stained with ash, as if frequently caught against protruding nails or brushed up against buckets of coal or scullery hearths.

The young lady's thick hair was swept up off her neck. Most of the dark locks were hidden not in a simple mobcap, but rather beneath a lovely bonnet—that appeared to have been worn to the Battle of Waterloo, so full of stains and holes was the fabric.

Fascinating headmistress.

Perhaps she had once been a lady's maid, and had subsequently fallen on hard times. A previous position in a wealthy home would explain the gloves and the gown and the bonnet. Losing that position would explain the rest.

Mostly.

Her porcelain skin was smooth and untouched by the bronzing rays of the sun. Her cheekbones were defined enough to give her face a quite attractive shape, but not so stark as to imply bouts of hunger or malnutrition, as was so often found in poverty-stricken areas. Her dark brown eyes were long-lashed and so luminous in the candlelight that he almost didn't notice the purple smudges beneath them, indicating it had been a long time since last she got a restful night's sleep.

As he watched, the edges of her perfect lips quirked and her eyes seemed to sparkle. "Well? Have you figured me out yet?"

"Not yet," he admitted. "But I think I'd like to."

Her smile widened. "My name is Miss Grenville. I

am the headmistress of this school. I owe you my deepest gratitude for attempting to catch tonight's villain."

"Attempting to?" he asked drolly.

"No one could blame you for losing him in the maze of alleys," she assured him. "To be honest, I didn't expect you to return at all."

"Then it is you who have not yet figured me out," he informed her, "for I did catch him. He will not return for some time. Nor will your current watchman, I'm afraid."

"Oh?" She raised an eyebrow wryly. "Did St. Giles ever have a watchman?"

He bit back a sigh. Her cynicism was well-founded.

"You will tomorrow," he promised. "I shall see to it myself."

"How is it you have so much power?" The appraising look she gave him was skeptical at best. "Are you someone I should recognize?"

"It pains me to admit that in this neighborhood, you are unlikely to have seen many of us at all. Allow me to present myself." He tipped his hat. "I am Mr. Spaulding. I work as an inspector at Bow Street. And I am at your service."

"At *my* service?" she asked in a teasing tone. "Does this mean I will see you again, Mr. Spaulding?"

"I am at everyone's service," he clarified. "I work for the City of London, and my first duty is to its constituents. All of them."

She arched a brow. "Does that mean yes, I will see

you again, or no, you can now cross us off your list?"

An impertinent question...deserving of an honest reply.

This time, Simon took an extra moment to consider his answer. Miss Grenville was clever enough not to accept platitudes, and to see through Simon's heartfelt declaration to a superficial layer he hadn't even known he possessed.

No, he had not planned on seeing Miss Grenville again. If she happened to be in the street when he happened to ride by once or twice a month when his purposefully random route to or from work happened to include this neighborhood, then yes. They would cross paths.

Otherwise, no. Simon did not give preferential treatment. Nor did he allow distractions of any time to clutter up the orderliness of his life. He worked. And then he slept. And then he returned to work the next evening. Nights were when he was most alive.

When any of the myriad Quality ladies who called upon Bow Street had asked if they could see him again with the same arch look in their eyes, Simon's stock answer was that they knew where to find the magistrate's court, which was staffed with any number of officers more than qualified to investigate crimes.

But Miss Grenville was different.

For one, despite being geographically closer to his office than the fine houses in Mayfair, it was far easier for the Beau Monde to dispatch one of their many coaches with one of their many footmen to drop a note off with the secretary.

For two, unlike the high society wives who thought it would be amusing to have a flirtation with a Runner, Miss Grenville had not asked if she would see him again because she believed there was a chance she might. Miss Grenville had asked if she would see him again because she assumed she would not.

She wanted him to admit the truth.

He would simply create another.

"Yes," he said firmly. "It is quite possible you will see me again, because I plan to take this route home every morning this week. Once I am certain the new watchman is performing his duty, I will resume my regular rotation. But for this week at least, if you happen to be out-of-doors when I pass by... I shall be certain to tip my hat."

"You should knock." Miss Grenville glanced over her shoulder. "I sent Molly to bed early tonight for obvious reasons, but I am certain she, too, would like an opportunity to thank you. Especially when I tell her you've caught the blackguard who attacked her."

"Nothing special," he said, shifting his weight to deflect the compliment. "I was just doing my duty."

"It was very special," she corrected with a smile that didn't quite reach her eyes. "No one in Molly's life had ever once stood up to protect her. Today would have been no different. Except tonight, she had me...and you."

He opened his mouth, but couldn't quite wrestle the words from his heart to his tongue.

"Good night, Mr. Spaulding." With a wink, Miss Grenville blew out her candle and shut the door.

Simon remounted his horse in somewhat of a daze. He hadn't promised to call upon the school tomorrow, but after that speech about no one ever having protected Molly before, how could he not?

Just one week, he told himself. He'd call tomorrow and ride by the next day without stopping. Once the new watchman was in position, Simon's protection would no longer be needed.

He need never have uncomfortable conversations with Miss Grenville again.

Chapter 3

Simon had *meant* to stop by the school on his way to work the following afternoon. After all, it was less than a mile from his office, which made it practically right on his path.

Yet, somehow he found himself tying his horse to a post in the middle of the day, hours before he was expected in the office.

Since he had already promised Miss Grenville that he would visit, doing so as soon as possible was merely an expedient way to cross tasks off the list of today's responsibilities.

Not to mention the very logical reasoning that if the point was to speak to Molly, not Miss Grenville, then the only practical course of action was to arrive before the students were abed.

After all, Simon had no wish to have to call upon the school a third time, did he?

None of which explained why his no-nonsense stride from the street to the front door felt less like a Bow Street inspector interviewing yet another innocent victim, and more like a flustered gentleman paying an unexpected call upon a lady.

Balderdash.

Simon did not pay calls upon ladies. Or anyone at all. He had no time for idle fraternization.

Not because he disliked people—quite the opposite. He dedicated his life to rescuing them. Bringing them justice. Keeping them safe. Watching over them from a quiet, impartial distance.

Yet some circumstances called for a more personable approach. That was it. He was just an officer, paying a one-hundred-percent work-related call. No hidden motive beyond speaking with the victims.

One of which had brained her attacker senseless with nothing more than a humble broom.

Simon adjusted his cravat. Whether Miss Grenville was a spitfire remained to be seen.

The door swung open. Just as the night before, no butler or housekeeper attended callers, but rather the headmistress herself.

Simon bowed. "Good afternoon, Miss Grenville. I trust the rest of your evening passed much more peacefully?"

"I'll send for Molly at once," she said without curtseying. Her eyes twinkled. "I thank you for both your service and your punctuality. She has been looking forward to your visit all day."

Before he could so much as blink, Miss Grenville motioned to a young girl in a frayed pinafore, who immediately raced up a somewhat lopsided staircase and disappeared into the next floor.

Miss Grenville turned back to him with a brisk nod. "There. She will be down any moment. We won't keep you long."

"She needn't rush," he found himself saying. "I've nothing but casework awaiting me."

Miss Grenville gave him a long, considering look.

Simon straightened. He had the distinct impression this young lady was taking his measure in the same careful, detailed way he had taught the other men on the force.

Something like: Hat, medium quality. Not rich, not poor. Hair, a bit too long—too much time between visits to the barber. Jaw, clean-shaven. Suit, waistcoat, cravat, well-tailored and pristine. He was an inspector, not a beadle or a street watchman. And he had returned, just as he'd promised.

"Forgive me." Miss Grenville dropped a curtsey elegant enough to rival a duchess. "We have just finished lessons, and I'm afraid my mind was with administrative responsibilities, and not on my manners."

Simon could scarcely fault her for a trait his colleagues would claim he himself had perfected, so he merely tipped his hat. "There is nothing to forgive. A strong focus on one's duty is a worthy quality indeed."

"Is it? 'Twould be better if I could do less focusing, more *achieving*, but, well… Someday, things will turn around. I would invite you to tea, but we don't often take it." She pushed the door open wider. "But you can still come in. As long as you aren't expecting crumpets."

"I despise crumpets," he assured her. "Ghastly things. Make me sneeze worse than cats."

"Well, if you ever find yourself with a surplus, I am certain my girls will be happy to dispose of them for you."

"Duly noted," he promised, and stepped across the threshold.

The interior of the school in many ways resembled Miss Grenville's wardrobe. One need only look past the worn edges and superficial damage to recognize the beauty beneath.

Although the gilt had long been stolen from the moldings, nothing could hide the original abbey's magnificent structure, the stunning artistry, the welcoming openness.

Laughter filled the air, ringing joyfully through the rafters as dozens of booted feet tiptoed down the stairs in unison.

"I sent for *Molly*," Miss Grenville scolded her charges, without bothering to hide her wide smile. "Not the rest of you meddling wretches."

"We *all* want to see the Runner," one of the girls said

gleefully. "Molly says he rescued her!"

Although the officers at Bow Street preferred to be thought of as inspectors, not Runners, Simon saw no need to be priggish. Instead, he gave the entire staircase of pinafored girls a sweeping bow. "Merely doing my job, ladies. I am ever at your service."

"Wonderful." Eyes laughing, Miss Grenville turned her wagging finger toward Simon. "Now they'll all swoon over constables the way other ladies used to swoon over soldiers."

"Why isn't your waistcoat red?" asked one of the older girls. "Ain't that why Runners are called Robin Redbreasts?"

"That would be the Horse Patrol, miss," Simon explained. He doubted scarlet-accented patrolmen were frequently spotted in this neighborhood. "I'm afraid inspectors do not wear a uniform."

"Gold waistcoats is nicer than red anyway," another girl said with a deep blush.

"Now, now," Miss Grenville interrupted. "As handsome as he is, Mr. Spaulding isn't here to flirt with you. Where's Molly? She's the reason for this visit."

Simon was careful not to display his pleasure at the realization Miss Grenville thought him handsome. He affected a serious expression. As she rightfully pointed out, he was not here for flirtation. The sooner he returned to his desk, the better.

"I'm here," a girl called out at the top of the stairs.

As she picked her way through the pack, Simon took

in the whole picture.

The boarding school appeared to have a solid foundation, but little money. Molly was clearly not a special case amongst the students. Miss Grenville's charges were indigent inhabitants of a rookery, not the offspring of wealthy families.

What a worthy cause. He could not help but admire Miss Grenville's pluck and protective instincts.

The only other institutions that might welcome these children were workhouses and orphanages—both of which were notorious for being little improvement over life on the street. A sobering percentage of their dependents never reached adulthood.

When Molly reached the foot of the stairs, she clasped her hands together and bobbed an awkward curtsey, as if it were one of the first occasions of her experience in which social propriety might require such a thing.

"Thank you," she said breathlessly. "If you hadn't rescued us from that awful man, ma'am wouldna rescued me from my awful life."

"She rescued me, too!" called one of the girls from the crowd upon the stairs.

"Rescued all of us!" shouted another.

"If you hadna come by when you did," Molly continued quietly, "I know what that man was goin' to do. He told me."

Simon forced his anger below the surface. He knew

precisely how that malefactor had intended to treat this young girl. If it were up to Simon, men like that would never be released from gaol.

Molly took a deep breath. "I understand men like him. But I didn't know what *you* was going to do. I never met a Runner before."

His heart thumped as he struggled for the right words to say.

"I didn't 'spect you to come back—no constable *ever* comes back—but when ma'am says you stopped by, just as you promised… Last night, I didn't believe her when she says good men do exist." Molly stared up at him with shimmering eyes. "Today, I do."

Simon swallowed the lump in his throat. "It is my hope that from this day forward, your life is full only of goodness." He glanced up at the rest of the girls. "You deserve it. All of you."

"Thank you." Molly blushed and ran back into the crowd of girls.

"That's enough distraction for one day." Miss Grenville made shooing motions at the children. "Back to your studies. You've much to do before supper."

"Goodbye, Runner!" one of the girls called over the handrail.

"I like your waistcoat, too!" yelled another, causing the rest to explode into cackles of laughter.

The entire group thundered up the stairs in a cloud of pinafores and giggles.

"They'll curtsey next time," Miss Grenville promised him. "We're still working on 'taking our leave.'"

"Are you?" he asked, more seriously than he intended. "Is this the sort of finishing school that focuses on the different types of curtseys and how best to flutter one's painted fan?"

"Not in the least," she responded cheerfully. "Most of these girls are unlikely to ever own a painted fan, much less curtsey to a queen. Our school is far more practical."

"In what way?" he asked, intrigued. "What subjects do they learn?"

Miss Grenville gave him a coy smile. "Come back some time. Before three. You'll catch them in their lessons."

"I...wouldn't want to interrupt," he said. Not just lessons—his meticulously planned, carefully ordered life. He lived by a strict schedule for a reason.

Every moment he spent with people who didn't need him took time away from those who did.

Miss Grenville was undeniably appealing. Her students were charming. But this would have to be goodbye.

"I see." Miss Grenville's eyes lost some of their sparkle. She had not needed him to enumerate his reasons to understand that he would not be back. "Before you go, I too would like to thank you. Not just for last night, but for today. You were very good with the children. Have you some of your own?"

"No." His answer came out more forcefully than intended. "I am unwed."

The dark brow she arched was meant to be ironic. From dukes to paupers, "marriage" was hardly a prerequisite to spawning offspring. Some were simply more circumspect about it than others.

Simon felt differently.

London already had more than enough unwanted children, without Simon adding to the problem. He wouldn't start a family unless he could *be* a family. A proper one, with both parents at home and plenty of time for the children.

However, none of that was in the cards. Every moment of every day was already spoken for. When the city no longer needed inspectors and constabulary, perhaps then he would reconsider. But for as long as he did more good on the streets, saving lives, catching criminals…

His life was more than full. And he had dallied here long enough.

"Good luck, Miss Grenville." He bowed, and stepped out onto the front step. "If you or your students need anything at all, Bow Street is a short distance away."

"Goodbye, Mr. Spaulding," she replied softly as she shut the door. "Keep rescuing people."

"I will." With determination, Simon adjusted his hat, mounted his horse, and set off to do exactly that.

Chapter 4

Simon tossed his hat onto the corner of his desk and glared at the scraps of paper littering the mahogany surface. Each square of parchment bore his small, precise hand. Notes. Details. Clues. Questions.

An insidious thief was loose in Mayfair, and he was no closer to solving the mystery.

He frowned. It had taken months to determine that a crime was even being committed.

In a room full of riches, only one small object would be stolen. Something easily concealed in a trouser pocket. Something unlikely to be missed. Something of more sentimental value to its owner than its comparative worth.

But the thief was not coldhearted. He chose an item of sentimental value not in an attempt to bring pain to the owner, but to ensure the object's safe return.

Within twenty-four hours of being pawned for cash,

an anonymous missive would arrive, informing the owner his lost object could be retrieved for a paltry sum at varying pawnshops.

The person who pawned it, however, was not so easily found. Street beggars were paid to make the exchange. The same faces were never seen twice. The thief was a ghost.

Simon ran a frustrated hand through his hair.

In some cases, the owner didn't even realize an item was missing until he received instructions on how to retrieve it. In every case, the monetary value of the stolen items was so inconsequential to their wealthy owners that reporting the crime rarely crossed their minds. His notes only contained a few documented cases.

If Simon did not possess a compulsion to protect and serve *all* people, he would be tempted to lower the priority of this case to the bottom of the pile.

London was brimming with real problems. People robbed of their lives, their innocence, their last penny, their last hope.

But right was right, and wrong was wrong. Just because the wealthy victims could afford their loss did not mean a crime should go unpunished. Someone needed to stop the Thief of Mayfair. And that someone was Simon Spaulding.

He dipped his pen into the inkwell and began transcribing the details of the case in a fresh way.

Instead of grouping each known crime chronologically, he began to create individual lists. A list of stolen items, a list of the rooms they were stolen from, a list of the pawn shops and their characteristics, a list naming and describing all the victims, a list of the monies received for each stolen good.

Somewhere in all this data was a clue he could use. A trick to predict the next robbery. A way to catch the criminal.

"Spaulding, did you hear me? It's half six. Join us for a drink before we go home?"

Simon glanced up to see the daytime inspectors hovering impatiently just outside the door to his office. Every evening at half six, they put on their hats and headed out for an after-work drink. Every time, they invited Simon to join them.

And every day he said no.

"I'm busy," he said, jabbing his pen back into the inkwell. He had just arrived for the night shift and was already buried in casework.

Perhaps he wouldn't be so busy if the other inspectors didn't trade the office for the pub every evening at half six. Then again, perhaps they wouldn't feel compelled to do so if the city would grant funding to hire a few more investigators.

"Suit yourself," the other officers murmured, as they did every time. "You know where to find us."

He did indeed. But Simon needed his mind to stay sharp. When working twelve hour days from dusk to dawn, clear thinking was the only way to do his job.

Besides, Simon didn't need sleep. Not when the city needed *him*. He didn't get drowsy when the sun went down. He came *alive*.

Criminals might believe they owned the darkness, but Simon Spaulding was the Lord of Night. At the end of the day, no felon could hide from justice.

"Inspector?"

Simon glanced up to realize another hour had slipped by. The office was empty, save for the secretary—who had a wife and small child he ought to get home to. "What is it, Mr. Webb?"

"Footman just dropped this off for you, sir." The secretary handed Simon a sealed document. "It's from the Justice of the Peace."

"Splendid." With a sigh, Simon broke the seal.

The Justice of the Peace frequently sent politically motivated missives to the department. Round up the prostitutes, the vagrants, the poor. Clean up London's streets.

This one had a different target.

"It appears that Lady Pettibone's nephew has taken to frequenting what she suspects to be an illegal gaming hell," Simon informed his secretary. He gave a sardonic smile. "His Honor believes that I alone am inspector enough to ensure Lady Pettibone's nephew loses his fortune in *legal* gentlemen's clubs."

"Well…" Mr. Webb's encouraging expression was devoid of irony. "You *are* the best investigator in the entire history of the department."

"It's not an old department," Simon muttered. "Don't we have real cases to solve?"

"It's a direct order from the Justice of the Peace," Mr. Webb pointed out. "You can't say no."

Shaking his head, Simon pushed to his feet. "I know."

Mr. Webb hesitated. "You must investigate the matter, but you needn't start tonight. If you don't have plans for supper, Mrs. Webb is cooking a goose in honor of our son's birthday."

"It sounds like a family affair." Simon reached for his hat and snugged it down to his ears. "Go home and enjoy your goose. The sooner I investigate this gambling establishment, the sooner I can return to my other cases."

Mr. Webb nodded and turned away.

Simon doubted his secretary had expected to be taken up on his offer. It was not the first time Mrs. Webb had cooked a goose or a pigeon or learned a new sauce. He had no doubt the invitations were sincere and the meals toothsome.

But if Simon had no free time for a family of his own, he had even less call to intrude upon someone else's.

He exited Bow Street and set out for the direction listed in the Justice's missive.

The address was right at the edge of the fashionable district. The club was not quite close enough to St.

James's Street to be confused with White's or Brooks's, but more than far enough from the rookeries to be considered a respectable location.

Simon observed the nondescript brick building carefully. The gaming den was called the Cloven Hoof. Run by one Maxwell Gideon, history unknown.

Unlike most public houses, the door was unopened. No sound could be heard from outside. He tied his horse to a post and rapped firmly on the closed door.

It opened a crack.

"Wrong knock," said a gruff voice. "Don't recognize you."

"I am not surprised," Simon said, suddenly more interested in the case. A man with nothing to hide would not hire an enforcer to keep potential customers out. "This is my first time here. Do allow me inside."

The door did not budge. "Who are you?"

"I am Mr. Simon Spaulding. Who are you?"

"Vigo," came the answering growl. "And unless you know the knock or someone vouches for you, you're not coming in."

Something gave Simon the impression that "knowing" a Justice of the Peace was not the sort of connection Vigo was looking for.

"Does Maxwell Gideon own this establishment?" he asked instead.

"Do you know Gideon?" Vigo countered skeptically.

Another tack, then. Simon affected a clueless grin.

"Lady Pettibone's nephew promised—"

"*Egbert*," the enforcer spat in disgust. "Always sending his Cambridge prats here."

The door swung open to reveal a large, burly gentleman with a resigned scowl.

"At least you culls are good for the money," the enforcer muttered as he gestured for Simon to enter. "Games up front near the bar, private tables in the back."

"What's the correct knock, for next time?" Simon asked innocently.

With a roll of his eyes, the enforcer's scarred knuckles rapped out a two-one-two pattern on the doorjamb.

"I'll try to remember," Simon murmured, and stepped inside.

The interior of the Cloven Hoof was dark, but cozily so. Cleverly placed mirrors refracted light from low-hung chandeliers with unusual efficiency.

A long, simple bar to the left separated the stores of alcohol from the gamblers who imbibed it. Behind the counter was a single barmaid, who poured drinks with a cheerfulness not usually found in such establishments.

To the right were the gamblers. Green felt Faro tables covered in chips. Hazard tables with flying dice. Plain wooden tables with clumps of men playing whist, casino, piquet, speculation.

"You lose!" squealed a man in dandified clothes as he gathered a stack of chips. "I'm going to buy *so* many actresses with this money... There's absolutely nothing they won't agree to do!"

"Shut it, Mapleton." A man in lesser finery shrugged off his greatcoat to expose his shirtsleeves as if the temperature in the club has suddenly increased. "You won this hand, not the night. It's my turn to deal."

Simon walked past the bar and the gaming tables to the rear half of the establishment. Here were the private tables the enforcer had referred to, though they were currently empty. In the back was a single closed door marked *Office*.

These sorts of establishments usually came in one of two flavors. Either they were exclusive gentlemen's clubs catering solely to the titled and very rich—the sort that Lady Pettibone undoubtedly expected her nephew to frequent would never have allowed someone as low-born as Simon to enter—or they were seedy underground gaming hells, where whatever money one failed to lose at the rigged tables would be just as efficiently pickpocketed before leaving the premises.

The Cloven Hoof appeared to be neither of these things.

The loud-mouthed dandy at the Faro table had been wearing an embroidered waistcoat so fine, it must have cost twice Simon's annual salary. On the other hand, the rest of the patron clearly were not Quality. No matter how warm the room, a true gentleman would never expose his shirtsleeves in public.

Indeed, Simon was far better tailored than a fair percentage of the dice-throwers and whist-players. Which was probably why the door enforcer had believed Simon to be an old university friend of Lady Pettibone's spoiled nephew.

He stepped back into the shadows as a distant office door swung open. His blood cooled.

The handsome, well-dressed blond gentleman who stepped out from the office was definitely not Maxwell Gideon.

It was Lord Hawkridge.

Simon's half-brother.

He sucked in a shocked breath and slid down into a dark corner table.

Not that Simon expected Hawkridge to have any clue who he was. But now that he'd determined he was in the midst of a true investigation, he could not risk giving away his true identity so soon.

If he could have had his way, he wouldn't recognize Hawkridge either.

Once Simon had determined to make his own way in the world, he'd gone out of his way to learn as little as possible about the half-brother who didn't even know he existed. It was the only way to save his sanity.

As an investigator, it would have been easy to torture himself with researching every tiny detail about the marquess's marvelous life. Simon had refrained. If anything, it had become an obsession *not* to investigate anything unrelated to active casework.

Besides, even if he'd wanted to, he didn't have time. London had more than enough footpads and gangs on the loose for Simon to waste time peering into the private lives of ordinary citizens.

Except when he had nowhere else to look because the man was right in front of him on the other side of the room.

Lord Hawkridge didn't even look Simon's way. His gaze was on the tall, dark gentleman stepping out of the office and locking the door.

Simon straightened. *That* must be Maxwell Gideon.

Conversing in low voices, the two men strode up front to the main area and disappeared out of view.

Simon's skin danced with nervous energy. *Now* what?

The only way out of the establishment was through the front door, which would mean walking past everyone in the main room. He would have to wait.

Quickly, he found a table with a better view of the front gaming salon, and nestled himself in the shadows to observe the others.

It was already torture.

He could scarcely think about Maxwell Gideon or the Cloven Hoof when all he could see was the expensively tailored profile of Lord Hawkridge.

Although they had both been sired by the same marquess, they had been raised in separate circles. Lord Hawkridge's mother was a marchioness.

Simon's had been nothing more than a mistress.

As he watched, Gideon murmured something. Because Simon's only view was to the back of Hawkridge's head, he could not gauge the reply.

Whatever the marquess said caused the club owner to burst into laughter and wave a swarthy hand in the direction of the bar.

Simon tried not to hate his brother. Had spent the last two-and-thirty years trying not to blame the son for the crimes of the father.

But it wasn't easy.

How many times had Simon thought his circumstances would have been so much easier if he hadn't known who his father was? If he had never so much as glimpsed his brother?

But of course he knew. How could he not? His brother's name was listed in *Debrett's Peerage*, right next to everyone else who mattered: Zachary Nash, Lord Hawkridge.

Absent from *Debrett's Peerage*: Simon. And his mother.

How Simon had *longed* for his father to acknowledge him, to be proud of him. He didn't want to be marquess; he knew he couldn't. Simon just wanted to have a few of the same things his brother did. To sail toy boats on the lake. To go on a carriage ride in the park. To have ices on Berkeley Square.

He didn't want riches.

He just wanted his father's time.

Such a foolish wish could never be granted. His father was important. Simon and his mother were not. They could not be acknowledged publicly, because they were an embarrassment to the marquess and his *real* family. The ones who got carriage rides and sweet ices and sunny afternoons by the lake.

Simon and his mother, on the other hand, were to stay out of sight, out of town, out of the way.

You understand, the marquess would say. *Out of respect for my wife. And my son.*

As if Simon were not.

He watched, teeth clenched, as the barmaid brought over a glass of port and made some sort of eye-fluttering cooing comment at Hawkridge.

Men like that believed a rakehell lifestyle made them seem manly. Simon was proof of the opposite. Unwed sexual encounters had devastating consequences for everyone but the rake.

Gideon and Hawkridge rose from their chairs and made their way to the Hazard tables on the other side of the salon.

Simon pulled out his pocketwatch and growled in frustration. If the marquess intended to start a game of dice, that meant he wasn't planning to quit the Cloven Hoof any time soon.

As much as he preferred not to be in the same room with the man, Simon had already wasted a full quarter hour in the shadows and was not prepared to waste the rest of his night.

When he was a child, and he and his mother would accidentally passed little lord Zachary on the street or in the park, Simon's half-brother had always looked straight through him as if there were no spark of recognition at all.

At first, Simon had thought his highborn half-brother was ignoring him because he believed commoners were inconsequential.

His mother had gently explained that the marquess's real son literally had no idea who Simon was…because he truly was nobody.

From that day forward, Simon was determined to be *somebody*. He might never be important enough for recognition to flash in the marquess's eye, but he was bloody important to all the Londoners he and his colleagues helped every day. And he had much better things to do than stare at his half-brother from afar like he'd done when they were younger.

Simon's years of living in the shadows were over.

He pushed to his feet and strode past the Hazard table and out the front door without looking back.

Chapter 5

Two days had passed since Dahlia had seen Mr. Spaulding.

Perhaps the inspector continued to ride past the school once per day as promised. Perhaps he did not. Bow Street Runners were busy men. She had no business trying to monopolize even a fraction of his interest. Not when the entire city could use more men like Mr. Spaulding.

And yet, for the third afternoon in a row, her mind was focused not on the piles of unpaid accounts before her, but on what she might say if she saw him again.

Dahlia had never suffered the slightest hesitation to talking with people.

For better or for worse, her runaway mouth had always started conversations with everyone she ever met. Dukes, modistes, street sweepers, flower girls. She wouldn't have been able to open this boarding school were it not for her propensity to collect orphans and her fearlessness to beg her betters for donations.

And yet, with Mr. Spaulding, she'd suffered a peculiar reticence. She doubted it was because he was the first Runner of her acquaintance. She had shown no signs of shyness the first time she'd met an earl or a governess or a pie-maker.

Which meant there must be something about Mr. Spaulding that made him different from the rest. Something that made *her* different. Something that made her sit at her desk mooning out the front window rather than—

Dahlia leapt to her feet, heart pounding. He was here.

Sort of.

He was outside on his horse, staring at the school from the corner of his eye as if he weren't certain whether the abbey threshold was safe to cross.

If she hadn't been gazing out the window like a featherbrained ninny, she might not have seen him stop. In fact, he didn't even look as though he were staying!

Quickly, she raced down the uneven stairs, through the entryway, and out the front door, just in time to see him pick up his reins in preparation to leave.

"Halt, Police!" she shouted teasingly as she ran down the walkway to the horse posts.

"'Inspector,'" he corrected just as teasingly, and lifted his hat. "I wasn't certain if you were home."

She wasn't *home*, exactly. Home was with her family on the other side of town, but none of that was the point. "How did you plan to determine my presence without knocking upon the door, inspector?"

He gave her a cocky smile. "I believe I managed, don't you think?"

Her cheeks flushed as she imagined her inelegant flight out the door.

"*Touché*," she said. "But would knocking not have been easier?"

"I'm still not certain I should have stopped at all," he admitted. "I promised to ride past your school, not deliver crumpets to it."

"Crumpets!" she exclaimed. "You did not. Did you?"

He reached inside a leather saddlebag and pulled out a brown paper package secured with a bit of twine. "You'll have to open it to find out."

"But what of your cat-like sensitivity?" she asked, cradling the parcel to her chest. "Are these special crumpets that don't make you sneeze?"

"I sneezed over every last one of them," he informed her cheerfully. "And then I tied them up in brown paper for safekeeping."

"Incorrigible scamp," she scolded him. "What a horrid thing to tease."

He smiled. "If you don't want the scones…"

"I'll take them. But you're not invited to tea."

"I am much like your girls in that regard," he admitted. "I cannot recall the last time I stopped to take tea."

"Well, in that case," she said with a dramatic sigh. "I suppose we can invite you, just this once. Their first tea, your first tea… I might as well teach the lot of you how to do a proper pour."

He straightened his hat. "Can't. Too many open cases."

"Hopefully nothing violent." She shuddered.

He shook his head. "Not at the moment. Thieves, gaming hells, that sort of nonsense. Plenty to keep one busy. How about you? No further nocturnal incidents, I hope?"

"It's been delightfully quiet," she assured him. "The girls are back to their regular, rambunctious selves."

"And you?" he repeated, his blue eyes locked on hers. "Are you feeling back to normal?"

"I've never been normal," she said cheerfully. "If you haven't noticed that by now, you're not much of an inspector."

His wide lips curved into a grin. "I notice more than you might care to think."

"Oh?" She stepped forward, intrigued. "What have you noticed about me?"

He tilted his head. "You're stronger than you let on. And more frightened. You come from significantly more money than you currently wield, yet you participate in more direct labor than mere bashing assailants with broomsticks. You haul coal, you wash laundry, you tend the hearth. You are exceptionally aware of your environment. You have a big heart and terrible penmanship, largely because you're left-handed. You skip more meals than just tea, and you've curled your hair every day since the night we met."

Dahlia blinked. How on earth did he know she was left-handed? Or any of the other things? She was not at all certain she cared for him to notice so much. And yet… "What do you mean, I've curled my hair every day since the night we met?"

"When I first visited your school on the night of the attack, your lovely chestnut hair was tucked under your bonnet, save for a few flyaway tendrils that had escaped their pins. In the three days since, the only thing escaping your bonnet are perfect little ringlets. Since I have seen that your hair does not form such shapes naturally, I am left to conclude that you have styled it thus on your own."

"Clearly I style it that way. No one's hair grows in perfect ringlets. The real question is how you would know what I looked like yesterday, unless you glimpsed me with your own eyes."

"Ah." He smiled. "I said you were observant. Now you have caught me. I rode by yesterday, but had no excuse to stop. Today, I have crumpets. And the sneaking suspicion that the pretext would have worked much better if I had stopped myself from explaining it."

Dahlia couldn't help but smile. He hadn't simply

been thinking of her. He'd been thinking about all her students. A treat for them was a far quicker way to her heart than some meaningless trifle for her would have been.

"There is absolutely no way your gift will be received badly," she assured him. "My girls will be thrilled to have a proper tea. It will be their reward for spending an hour a day learning self-defense."

His eyebrows lifted. "Did you add that to the curriculum after the attack the other day?"

She shook her head. "It has always been an important part of their studies. Molly, however, was not yet a student at the time of the attack."

"Do you think it would have gone differently if she had been?"

"I hope it helps in the future. No amount of training will enable a young girl to overpower a grown man, but the element of surprise is powerful indeed. Sometimes a mere moment is all it takes to break free or scream for help. And now that they have each other, they no longer have to brave the streets alone."

His gaze softened. "It sounds like your school really is improving lives."

"Isn't that what we both strive for?" She smiled up at him. "Helping others, I mean?"

"It's the reason I wake up every morning," he said, his eyes serious. "And it reminds me that I've taken enough of your time. Go spoil your hungry girls, head-mistress."

She stepped back to give him room. "Go rescue a few fair maidens, Runner."

He tipped his hat. "None will be as fair as you."

Before she could answer, he rode off across the cobblestones, down past the dial tower and out of sight.

She stood there longer than was seemly, clutching a parcel of still-warm crumpets to her chest.

Chapter 6

Dahlia sat in the front parlor of the Grenville family townhouse and hoped that coming home hadn't been a mistake.

Within these walls, she'd learned to walk, to talk, to read, to dance, to tumble, to embroider, to perform sums...everything except the one thing she needed most.

Permission to speak with her father.

She set down her teacup and leaned forward. "Please, Mother. It is urgent that I speak with him. Can you not ask him for a moment of his time?"

"Absolutely not." Mother added another cube of sugar to her tea. "Your father is frightfully busy, darling. Barons are very important people. He hasn't time for daughters. That's what mothers are for. Aren't you enjoying this tea?"

Dahlia was not enjoying this tea.

The one she'd shared yesterday with two dozen delighted students had been infinitely more satisfying. Better yet, none of the girls had repeated the same well-worn platitudes Dahlia had heard since childhood.

Your father is frightfully busy, darling. Barons are very important people. He hasn't time for daughters.

Folderol. He was a baron, not a duke. Father held no seat in the House of Lords. He didn't even belong to a gentlemen's club.

If he could not make time in his schedule for a word with his daughter, then he was either too heartless to care about two dozen *other* girls…or else he had no idea that his daughters had spent the last five-and-twenty years begging for an audience with him.

"He should *make* time for his daughter," she bit out through clenched teeth, even though such an opinion would alienate her further from her mother. Dahlia slumped back against her wingback chair in defeat. Oh, why had she even bothered?

"None of your impertinence," Mother chided with a shake of her finger. "You were always the most headstrong of the litter, but it is now time to grow up."

Dahlia counted to twelve before responding. "Mother, I *am* grown. To your eyes, I may be the black sheep of this family, but to the students at my school, I am headmistress—and, frankly, nothing short of a miracle to them. They were good girls in bad situations. I am trying to give them a better one. How do you expect me to keep clothing and feeding them without the aid of donations?"

"I don't expect you to continue with that silly project at all. It is past time you do your duty and get married. Just think how much happier you'll be when you're settled. A husband might be talked into taking you, but no reasonable man can be expected to take on the debt of a school of unsavories."

"A school of—" Dahlia choked rather than repeat the phrase. "Ignoring every other offensive remark in that speech, can we please agree that the girls themselves are innocent?"

"Fine, if it will calm you down. Even those who live on the streets can be innocent. That does not mean I or anyone else is required to pay for them. The government funds hospitals and orphanages, Dahlia. That's where those children would be if they truly required care."

"Mother…" Dahlia rubbed her face with her hands. "Have you ever even *seen* an orphanage? Inside, where the children are?"

Her mother flashed her a baffled look before selecting another teacake. "Of course not. Why would anyone want to go there?"

"That's the point! *No one* would want to go there. Not you, not me, not any children I have ever met. And yet, I am not sneaking in the windows at night to whisk them away. The girls at my school weren't even fortunate enough to have a bowl of gruel and a lice-ridden mat on an orphanage floor. All they have is me. And to keep the school running—"

"I will not plague your father with a single word of this fancy. And that's final. Your father's portion is the precise amount this family needs, and I will not beggar my other children just to put bread in the mouths of your wards. Think about your sister. She also needs to make a fine match."

"My dowry, then," Dahlia suggested. With that, she could buy books for a library, pencils for doing sums, globes to practice geography. Food for the larder. "No one else is using my dowry money. Father could donate the funds to the school. It would pay for several months' expenses. Lives could depend on it."

"Over my dead body." Mother set down her tea plate. "You will use that money to attract a husband, and so help me, that poor man will take you as far from that ridiculous school as humanly possible."

Dahlia clenched her fingers. "It's not ridiculous at all. I'm teaching them things they need to know. Giving them skills they never had."

"Why on earth would ragamuffins require a finishing school? Does it matter if they can paint a watercolor or walk without slouching?"

"Absolutely not at all, Mother. You're exactly right. That's why I'm showing them practical skills. For example, there are no maids at the school. The girls not only tidy their own chambers, but are responsible for cleaning the entire abbey. Every week, they rotate to a new shift: chambermaid, scullery maid, lady's maid, downstairs maid. The eldest even take turns as head housekeeper."

"What is the point, Dahlia? That your little project is failing so badly you cannot even afford a maid-of-all-work?"

"The point is that many of those girls are now qualified to *be* a maid-of-all-work. They entered with no marketable skills, and they'll leave with a signed reference affirming them capable of a paid position. It may not sound like much to you, but believe me when I say it is life-changing for them."

Mother sighed and poured herself another spot of tea. "You wouldn't have to worry about money at all if your school were in a better neighborhood. I wouldn't have to be embarrassed when the topic comes up at dinner parties. If you started a *proper* finishing school, you could charge a self-sustaining tuition and attract a far better quality of girl. Wouldn't that be the best of all worlds?"

Dahlia clenched her fingers and counted to thirty. It was comments like these that most infuriated her about her mother. As much as Mother liked to play the role of henwitted baroness who left all the money and business thoughts to her husband, it was more than clear that she had a very sound idea indeed of how one might make money managing an upper crust boarding school.

Her objection wasn't to Dahlia's work ethic, but to her audience. Unfortunately for Dahlia's girls, such prejudice was often the case. For every duchess or viscountess who donated a stack of pound notes, ten other wealthy wives couldn't be bothered to part with a single guinea.

Their reasons for avoiding charity projects ran the gamut from *ladies don't talk about such things* to *not my problem*. Was it any wonder Dahlia had occasionally had to resort to desperate measures to make ends meet?

"Fine," she said, defeated. "If you won't let me speak to Father, I'll fund the school some other way."

Mother narrowed her eyes over her teacup. "If I hear one peep about you stealing half-eaten food from my friends' rubbish bins…"

"I was twelve years old when that happened," Dahlia reminded her without heat. "Far too young to understand propriety dictates we toss out perfectly good scraps of food and cloth and paper, rather than donate them to poor families who cannot afford them. Obviously we should toss our remnants into the slop bin, rather than feed the hungry."

"At least you've learned something," her mother said with a sniff. "Honestly, darling, I just want you to be happy. Won't you consider finding a nice man? I can help, if you like. If you marry a man with deep pockets, you won't ever have to worry about money again."

"I don't want a man with deep pockets," Dahlia snapped. "Not unless he wants to donate the majority of it to the poor. Otherwise, what good is he for the school? I'd rather a man with the time and heart to work beside me, than some rich nob who cannot part with a single ha'penny."

The inspector's handsome face came to mind. *He* would understand these arguments. Mr. Spaulding was as kind to her girls as if they were wards of his own. If he could spare a few moments in his busy day, why couldn't the wealthy part with a few farthings?

Mother sighed. "This would be so much easier if all you wanted was a viscountcy to manage. I am at least acquainted with a few of those. Why do you care so much about children you don't even know?"

"I want them to have options!" Dahlia burst out. "I want their futures to be up to *them*."

"Oh, darling." Mother set down her saucer with a sad smile. "I am not the enemy. When will you learn that none of us have ever had choices?"

Rather than respond, Dahlia pushed to her feet. "Don't wait up for me, Mother. I'll be spending the night at the school until I can be sure if its security."

"Please consider marriage," her mother replied without standing up. "And soon. Bryony cannot wed until you have done so. Now that Camellia has nabbed an earl, a precedent has been set. If you would just close the school and try to get back into Almack's, you might do as well as your sister."

"Goodbye, Mother. Enjoy the rest of your tea."

Dahlia made her way out of the parlor and up the familiar steps to the sisters' shared sitting room. Until recently, all three sisters were usually found within its sunny yellow walls. Dahlia, perched on the bay window. Bryony, either at the violin or attempting to curl her un-curlable hair. Camellia, practicing her scales or playing the unflappably calm intermediary between her two younger sisters.

Today, the room was empty. Bryony was God-knew-where, and Cam no longer lived at home. She had indeed married an earl, albeit a scandalous one. Although he and Dahlia had not started off on the right foot, her brother-in-law had recently pledged an eye-popping do-nation that was more money than any headmistress could hope to raise in six months.

But it still wasn't close to enough. The girls didn't need six months' respite. They needed years. They needed a childhood. They needed time to grow up and mature and learn. What was she going to do?

Dahlia plopped down onto the window seat and leaned her head against the glass.

Her sister had become even more scandalous than her infamous husband the day she'd joined the opera. Cam had promised to donate every cent of her earnings to Dahlia's school for as long as necessary, but she had to move up the ranks like every other incredible soprano.

Until she was a household name for reasons other than scandal, Camellia's salary wasn't enough for one person to live on, much less two dozen. Someday, she might earn enough to match her husband's generous do-nation. But that day was not yet here.

Dahlia slid down against the window cushion and

wished Cam was there. Not because she needed money, but because she missed her big sister. Camellia had always been as cherished a sounding board as Dahlia's best friend Faith.

A smile tugged at Dahlia's lips. She was fortunate to be surrounded by so many strong, smart women. With luck, Faith might even have time to help with the school. The trick would be convincing her to try.

The sitting room door banged open and a whirlwind spun into the room, violin in hand.

Bryony squealed in disbelief. "*Dahlia?*"

At the sight of her youngest sister, Dahlia's melancholy vanished. She sprang to her feet.

Bryony tossed her violin case onto the closest chaise as if the Stradivarius inside hadn't cost as much as their townhouse and enveloped Dahlia in a breath-stealing embrace. "How *are* you? How's your school? What are you doing here?"

"I'm fine," Dahlia said, laughing as her sister danced her about the room. "The school is about the same. I came to ask Father for money."

Bryony stopped dancing, her eyes huge. "Did he give it to you?"

"I didn't even get to ask," Dahlia said with a sigh. "A two-hour tea with Mother and the closest I got was, 'Your father is frightfully busy.'"

Bryony rolled her eyes. "Did she give you the 'Barons are important people' speech, too?"

Dahlia laughed humorlessly. "Why else would we be asking to speak to him?"

"I don't know how you stand it." Bryony flung herself onto the chaise opposite her violin. "I've never lasted for more than twenty minutes at one of Mother's insufferable teas. Too much speechifying."

"She means well. Or at least, she thinks she does." Dahlia sat on the floor and wrapped her arms about her knees. "Her arguments drive me positively mad, but as long as they mirror the views of half her friends…"

Bryony lifted a shoulder in commiseration. "Mother is Mother."

Dahlia nodded. "Mother *is* Mother. How about you? What were you out doing?"

"Lessons." Bryony grinned. "Now that Camellia's on her way to being a household name, I cannot bear to be thought of as the least talented Grenville offspring."

"No," Dahlia reminded her. "That would be me. The only unmusical Grenville. You've got your violin, Cam has her voice, Heath acquits himself well at the pianoforte, and I… What do I have to offer? I don't even have good enough handwriting to pen the invitations to the family musicales."

"It's because you're left-handed," Bryony said, reaching out to pat Dahlia on the shoulder. "You smear the ink as fast as you write it. I can see bits on your sleeve even now."

Dahlia inspected her ink-splattered sleeve and grinned. *Aha.* That was how Mr. Spaulding had guessed her terrible penmanship.

"What did you learn at your lesson?" she asked.

Bryony bolted upright with a smile. "Do you want me to play it for you?"

"More than anything."

Bryony sprang up from the chaise and readied her violin. In minutes, the sitting room was filled with a soaring, haunting melody that rose to a crescendo before dashing itself into minor chords and back again.

Of course it was incredible. Bryony was incredible. Dahlia's entire family was comprised of individuals who stood out from the crowd in meaningful ways.

As Mother had pointed out, barons were indeed important people. As were baronesses. And operatic sopranos. And phenomenal violinists, who could play an entire piece from memory after listening to it one time. Her brother Heath's skills weren't limited to the pianoforte.

And then there was Dahlia. A headmistress who couldn't write her own name without smearing it. Whose school was on the brink of financial disaster. Whose own mother believed her best hope for the future was to wed any man willing to take her.

Dahlia didn't just want her school to succeed. She *needed* it to. She knew what it felt like to feel talentless and useless and dependent only on the whims of others, and she never wanted her students to have to feel that way ever again.

When the music ended, Bryony lowered her bow. "Well? What did you think?"

"It was hideous," Dahlia lied, earning a pillow cushion to the face. "Positively undanceable."

Bryony bounced in delight. "Speaking of dancing... Are Heath and I coming back this Saturday?"

"Absolutely. I promised the girls an hour lessons every week. Don't you dare make a liar of me."

"I wouldn't dream of it." Bryony slid her violin back into its case. "It's too bad there's no pianoforte. Heath is splendid with minuets."

"I need him to be splendid on the dance floor," Dahlia reminded her. "He's the only gentleman I trust to stand up with them. If I could afford a real dance-master..."

Bryony's face fell. "I spoke to my solicitor. You know I would give you every single penny I could, but the terms of my current long-term investment are immutable."

Dahlia had no idea what any of Bryony's mysterious investments were, but it was a relief that she couldn't get her hands on the money. Unlike Camellia, Bryony wasn't married to an earl who would take care of her, even if she donated all her money to her sister's barmy project.

Bryony would hand over every penny out of love for her sister, but Dahlia didn't need a loan. She couldn't pay anyone back. The donations weren't financial investments—they were *personal* investments. Into the futures of two dozen little girls who, without the school, would either die on the streets…or wish they were dead.

Dahlia would never have started her school if she'd thought her wards' futures would be in jeopardy. Before the school first opened, she'd had a full year's expenses in her account, plus hundreds of pounds of promised donations on the way.

Unfortunately, the careless words of a fashionable earl made her project suddenly unfashionable. What had once seemed like a more than adequate financial buffer had slowly drained through her fingers until there was nothing left. Her outrage at the earl's casual destruction was the only emotion that outweighed her panic.

In desperation, she had pilfered one of his meaningless baubles during a dinner party and pawned it to buy food for her wards.

Was stealing right? It was not. But she wasn't sorry. He had nearly cost two dozen girls their homes. If nicking a cufflink here and there stopped that from happening while she frantically worked to come up with a better plan… Well, Dahlia would have to do what she had to do.

"Don't worry," she said. "I'll find a way."

"I could sell my shoes," Bryony suggested. "And my fur muff. You're welcome to anything in my wardrobe you could exchange for a shilling."

Dahlia shook her head. She had already raided her siblings' wardrobes. And their old nursery. And the rag bin. If she sold much else, the entire family would be barefoot. And Dahlia's mother would cut her off for good.

Years ago, it had been Bryony who had begged for an audience with their father. She wanted to invest. To buy and sell stocks.

Mother had all but slapped her face for such an appalling suggestion. Bryony's talent for mathematics was both a curse and an embarrassment to the family.

Rather than lose her temper as Dahlia would likely have done, Bryony had simply begun pawning anything she owned of value. The jewelry went first, followed by any number of "useless baubles" that came her way for her birthday and other holidays.

At one point, Bryony had claimed to have "riches." Both Cam and Dahlia had doubted that very much— what were "riches" to a young girl who had no expenses?—but shortly thereafter, Bryony's investments became large enough that they could not be performed without a solicitor. Months later, the entirety of her funds was tied up in a project so mysterious she refused to breathe a word to her own sisters.

Worst case scenario, Bryony was being taken advantage of. Best case scenario, there was no project, and Bryony had fallen in love. Dahlia would be not at all surprised if Bryony were to announce she intended to run away with her solicitor or some East India magnate.

She would just be sad to say goodbye to another sister so quickly after losing Cam.

A knock sounded on the sitting room door.

Dahlia frowned.

A servant would have entered. A guest would have been announced.

She stood and made her way to the door. "Who is it?"

No one answered.

She narrowed her eyes. Ha. There was only one person who could have come to call. In one fluid movement, she flung open the door and leapt out of reach.

Her brother Heath barreled into the room, shoulder forward in a tackle that would have taken her down—if she'd been foolish enough to be standing in the way.

Instead, Dahlia hooked her foot under his ankle and gave him a sharp push to skew his forward trajectory sideways.

Rather than splat to the floor, Heath dropped in a single smooth somersault, springing to his feet with his palms facing her direction. She had less than a second to adjust her stance before his arms caught her right in the midsection, spinning her up and over his shoulder like pirate claiming his prize.

Quickly, she hooked her arms about his neck in a headlock and let herself fall backward, deadweight, until he was forced to his knees.

"*Good* one," Heath choked out with obvious pride. "It's been months since I've bested you."

Dahlia loosened her hold on her brother's neck in

exchange for a heartfelt embrace. "Years, puppy. I should be giving *you* lessons in self-defense."

Bryony glanced up from buffing her fingernails. "Why can't you ever just shake hands? Normal people shake hands."

"Nobody shakes hands," Heath protested in mock offense. "Smart people bow or curtsey. Shaking hands is the quickest way to getting flipped arse over teakettle."

"Normal people don't flip other normal people arse over teakettle," Bryony pointed out. "Why don't you two join the circus where you belong?"

"Actually," Dahlia interrupted, taking her brother's hands. "I was hoping you could stay after dance class on Saturday and show the girls better self-defense techniques. I've been teaching them all that I can, but it's hard to illustrate proper moves without two people to demonstrate."

Heath's smile faded. "Unfortunately, that's why I'm here. Something has come up. I'm no longer free on Saturdays."

"What about Sundays?" Dahlia asked. "There really isn't a set schedule. Any time you can squeeze in a few hours at the school, the girls will be more than happy to—"

"I can't," he said firmly. "Not right now. I promise to let you know if that changes."

Dahlia's spirits fell. Her brother always had time for her. Whatever had come up must be important, indeed. She forced herself to nod her acceptance.

Perhaps this was good news. Only a churlish wretch would worry she was about to lose her brother so soon after losing a sister.

"It's fine," she assured him. "I'll figure something out."

Bryony frowned. "Do you still want me to drop by the school?"

"*Please*," Dahlia said. "The girls deserve a little music in their lives. They love it when you play for them."

But it wouldn't last forever, she realized suddenly. Bryony had dreams of her own. And the day she stopped coming…

The music would be gone.

Chapter 7

Simon secured his horse outside the St. Giles School for Girls and strode confidently to the door. He was not some errant knight bringing flowers to his lady. He was a paid inspector doing his job. Nothing more.

After the attack in the alley, he had promised Miss Grenville to pass by the school every day for a week. He had done so. All was well. There was no reason to keep coming 'round. He was merely calling one final time to let her know.

He rapped sharply on the front door.

It swung open to reveal not the woman he had expected, but rather a familiar child with freckled cheeks and plaited hair. "Molly?"

"I can't curtsey," she whispered. "Today I ain't a maid, but a butler."

"A butler," Simon repeated, thoroughly confused. "Here I thought you were a pupil."

"Sometimes," Molly agreed. "But is anyone ever only one thing? Don't yet have 'nough experience to take my turn as head housekeeper, but I want to help Miss Grenville as much I can. Up 'til now, she's the one who's been headmistress and butler. See no reason why we can't take shifts, d'you?"

"I…" Simon cleared his throat and began anew. "Is your previous butler at home? I've come to speak with her."

"She's in the back salon finishing up lessons. This way."

Although he hadn't intended to cross the threshold at all, Simon found himself following the pinafored underbutler past the entryway and the warped marble stairs to a large open chamber at the rear.

A score of panting, giggling schoolgirls lay in sweaty heaps on the scuffed wooden floor, as if they had just finished running the most amusing mile of their lives.

Miss Grenville stood up on a dais at the far end of the open salon.

Wearing *trousers*.

"I…" He meant to announce himself. Truly, he did. But his throat would not make sounds, and his eyes could not tear away from the sight

"Mr. Spaulding!" she said warmly, as if there was nothing at all unusual about a headmistress standing on a dais in trousers whilst surrounded by a sea of exhausted schoolgirls. "What a marvelous surprise. Just one moment, if you please."

Simon could do nothing but watch helplessly as she unlooped a belt from a clump of fabric at her hips, sending the extra material clumped about her waist billowing down to her ankles. It was a day dress.

No sign of the trousers remained.

Nonetheless, Miss Grenville slipped behind a folding screen off to one side of the dais, leaving Simon to wonder—nay, agonize—over the enticing possibility that she was even now unbuttoning the fall of her shocking trousers, easing the fabric down over her bare hips, over the curve of her arse, over black lace garters circling her thighs, over her smooth, silk-stockinged calves to her shapely ankles... His breath quickened.

"*There.*" Miss Grenville stepped back into view, looking as fresh and normal as any pretty young woman who under absolutely no circumstances would even consider wearing trousers. "Girls, did you curtsey to Mr. Spaulding?"

A few straggled to their feet, whilst the others moaned variations of, "I'm tiiiired..."

"Up, up, up," Miss Grenville said briskly. "Exercise is good for the soul. Especially since our Saturday dance lessons have been suspended until further notice."

"*What?*" All the previously too-exhausted-to-curtsey schoolgirls sprang to their feet in protest. "But I love dance lessons! Why did you cancel them?"

"I haven't canceled them. Your dancing-master has

simply gone on holiday. Lessons will be resumed as soon as he returns, or we find a suitable replacement. Mr. Spaulding, I don't suppose you can dance?"

"I…" Simon stammered, too intoxicated by his vision of Miss Grenville sensuously removing her trousers to process anything else that was happening. "Of course I can dance."

"Prove it." She strode through the sea of wide-eyed schoolgirls, stopping an arm's reach away to consult an imaginary object on her wrist. "Let's see, if I could just make out the next name on my dance card…"

She was in his arms before Simon even realized he was stepping forward. He swung her out in a dramatic arc, then back into his embrace, such that her back was flush to his chest with her arms crossed about her waist.

"It doesn't matter whose name is on the card," he murmured into her ear. "This is my dance."

The pulse point jumped at the base of her throat and her beautiful lips parted. "I'm yours. Show me."

He twirled her so that she faced him, and positioned himself at a far more respectable distance than he would have preferred. "Can you waltz?"

"Can you?" She arched a brow as she placed her hand in his.

He curved his hand about her waist and led her in sweeping, dramatic circles, keeping time to the orchestra thundering solely in his mind. The steps, he knew by heart. The dance, he'd performed a thousand times.

But never like this. Never with her. His pulse thudded.

"Are you still wearing your trousers?" he asked, keeping his voice low.

"You're an inspector." Her eyes twinkled at him. "Inspect."

He slid his hand ever so slightly lower down the small of her back. Beneath his fingers was the silk of her dress, the thin cotton of the shift beneath…and no sign of the thick waistband that would have been holding up her trousers.

She'd taken them off. His imagination was right. Now, underneath her gown…she wore nothing.

"Have you concluded your investigation?" she asked with a teasing smile.

"I prefer to keep it wide open," he replied, his voice hoarse. "There are always secrets to unveil."

A flash of pink, as her tongue peeked out to lick her lips.

Before he could do something so foolish as haul her to his chest and kiss her in front of an entire salon of tittering schoolgirls, Simon spun Miss Grenville out of his arms and took a dramatic bow.

"I believe that's enough dancing," he said firmly.

Thunderous applause from their delighted audience drowned out most of his words.

"Dance lessons are Saturday evenings at eight," Miss Grenville said. "Will we see you then?"

"I'm very busy on Saturday evenings at eight," he

said with growing desperation. "I'm very busy...detecting."

She waved this objection away. "It's only for an hour."

"We can't. It's improper." Not dancing itself, but the unrestrained hunger he felt when he held her in his arms. If they had been anywhere but a school salon...

"We'll be chaperoned by none other my sister, who provides the music for the lesson. The previous dancing-master was my brother. The girls are quite used to the routine."

"What, precisely, is the routine?"

"You and I will demonstrate first. A country dance, a minuet, whatever Bryony feels like playing. After that, you and I both take the male parts in order to take turns partnering with each of the girls. You and I would only be dancing together once, at the very beginning."

Simon wasn't at all certain whether dancing with her only once made the offer better or worse.

"I really shouldn't make promises," he said. "I don't fraternize as a rule, and important cases could require my attention at any moment."

"That's easy enough. If you can come, come. If you cannot, send a note."

"Or crumpets!" shouted one of the girls. "We'll forgive anything for crumpets!"

"We shouldn't be alone," he whispered. "It isn't proper."

"I wouldn't dream of it." She fluttered her lashes up at him innocently. "Why, anything at all could happen."

Simon would make sure it didn't. For his own sake, as much as hers. "I'll come Saturday, but I make no promises after that."

She gave him a secretive smile. "Then I suppose it's up to me to make sure you keep coming."

Chapter 8

As soon as Mr. Spaulding was safely out the door, Dahlia collapsed against the other side and tried to catch her breath.

Good heavens, the man could dance. But she would be fooling herself if she tried to claim her runaway pulse was due to anything but the man she'd been dancing with.

Unlike most men of her acquaintance, Mr. Spaulding was impossible to figure out.

Most men of the ton fit into one of several broad categories. The rakes, the dandies, the Whigs, the Tories—whatever principal characteristics a man held were usually quite apparent from the first. Conversation tended to center solely on horseflesh, or politics, or gambling, or fashion, or any number of topics Dahlia cared very little about.

With Mr. Spaulding, however, she could not help

but feel she had barely scratched the surface of the complex man beneath.

On the one hand, he was a Bow Street Runner. There was nothing he hadn't seen. All of London's sins and dark corners surrounded every moment of his life. Depravity and wickedness surrounded him every day.

On the other hand, Mr. Spaulding was so rigidly proper that it took little effort at all to put a stammer in his words and a blush to his cheeks. The comical expression of horror on his face when he'd first glimpsed her wearing trousers...

Was nothing compared to the breath-stealing heat in his eyes when he realized she'd taken them off. Her pulse still pounded at the memory.

She hadn't realized how much she'd pushed him with her flirtations. She'd been poking a sleeping lion. Playing with fire. But the moment had been too perfect to pass up. He was so gentlemanly. So proper. The only reason he'd danced with her at all was because he'd been too flustered to say no.

If pushing him a little bit further got him to agree to be dancing-master, what was the worst that could happen?

Besides panting for breath in the vestibule of her school because a simple moment in his arms had robbed her of the ability to stand on her own legs.

A sudden knock rumbled against Dahlia's shoulder blades.

She flung open the door. "Mr. Spaulding!"

Dahlia's best childhood friend stared back at her with raised eyebrows and a bemused smile. "I'm afraid it's merely Faith Digby. The woman you sent for. Arriving as requested."

Dahlia burst out laughing and dragged her best friend into the school before Dahlia could embarrass herself further.

"Is Mr. Spaulding expected?" Faith asked. "Or was he just here?"

"Just here. He stopped by to..." Dahlia pressed her fist her mouth in horror. She'd flustered the poor man so much, he'd forgotten to mention why he'd come by in the first place. "Heath can no longer be dancing-master, I'm afraid. Mr. Spaulding has kindly agreed to take his place. At least on a trial basis."

Faith hung her pelisse on a hook. "I'm sure you can think of better uses for Mr. Spaulding's time. Why bother with dancing lessons?"

Dahlia cut her a sharp look. "You mean because these girls are unlikely to be sent invitations to any balls? I'm not grooming them for an official come-out. I just think that everyone deserves a little fun. If only for one hour per week."

Faith sighed. "I suppose I would feel more warmly about dancing as a pastime if anyone had stood up with me. I *did* have lessons and I *did* attend public assemblies, but no one ever asked. It was as much a waste of my time as finishing school was."

"This is not a finishing school," Dahlia reminded her. "It's a boarding school that teaches girls practical skills they'll use the rest of their lives."

"That's what my teachers said when they forced us to gad about balancing books on our heads to improve posture," Faith grumbled. "I can think of a hundred better uses for books. Like reading them."

"Unfortunately, we don't have any," Dahlia said. "If we did, I could teach the girls to read. I'm sure they would love books as much as you do." She looped her arm through Faith's and steered her toward the stairs. "Come on up to my office. I have a proposal I hope you'll like."

She smiled. "Where are the girls?"

"Resting in their rooms. It's been quite an exciting day."

Faith wiggled her eyebrows. "Mr. Spaulding?"

"Mr. Spaulding," Dahlia agreed reluctantly as she shoved her best friend into her private office and shut the door behind them. She'd mentioned him to Faith after he'd chased off Molly's attacker. And then mentioned him again after he'd surprised her with crumpets. "He's…"

"Mm-hmm," Faith murmured with a knowing smile. "I can see what he is."

"It's not what you think," Dahlia protested. "We have a…professional relationship."

Faith nodded. "I could tell by the way you flung open the door and almost kissed me."

"Mostly professional," Dahlia amended. Her cheeks heated at the memory of being in his arms. "He's just a dancing-master for the girls. I don't have time for anything more and neither does he."

"Does he have time at all? I thought he was a Bow Street Runner."

"He's a Bow Street Runner and a dancing-master for indigent girls. It's all the crack," Dahlia said with a straight face. "You should read the papers more."

Faith stretched out on an ancient chaise and locked her fingers behind her head. "He's a paragon, and I absolutely must meet him someday. But I assume you didn't summon me here to talk about Mr. Spaulding?"

Dahlia sobered and dropped to the worn carpet beside the chaise. "No. I need you, Faith. I can't do this alone."

Faith closed her eyes. "You need me, or you need my money?"

"Both," Dahlia answered baldly. "I've spent every penny of mine, and I'm hopeless at managing those details. My strengths lie with the students. I'm good at teaching, and motivating, and encouraging, and building excitement. I'm happy to knock on every door in London to beg for more funds, but the truth is I can't do it all anymore. I never could. I need help."

Lots of help. Dahlia's sister Bryony was too busy with her own affairs to take on another obligation. Faith's love of children was Dahlia's last hope.

"I hated boarding school," Faith said with a sigh. "I'll donate money, but why on earth would I want to help manage one?"

"To make it a *good* boarding school," Dahlia said passionately. "To make it a refuge, not a punishment. To make it an experience to cherish. To create an environment where the students are thrilled to take part, where every lesson truly prepares them for a better life."

Faith did not reply.

Dahlia leaned the back of her head against the chaise. "I'm trying to be the best headmistress I know how. My girls aren't debutantes. They're orphans and runaways and vagrants. Even if the school doesn't last a year, I don't want them to have to go back to the streets. I want to give them skills. Choices."

"Like what?" Faith asked after a moment.

"Everyone has maid duty two weeks per month," Dahlia said quickly. "They rotate through the abbey so they know how to clean bedchambers and hearths and chimneys."

Faith nodded slowly. "Not bad."

"Rather than French class, we have cooking class," Dahlia continued. "The girls take turns in both the scullery and the kitchen, where they learn to make breads, soups, tea cakes, pies—anything they could possibly sell on the street, or that might find them work in a bakery, if only washing dishes."

"I assume they do wash dishes?"

"They wash everything. Windows, floors, glasses,

vegetables. The school has no servants. We have students. They take six-day shifts being everything from footmen to chambermaids. And in their free time, I try to give them a little fun. Music. Dance. Everybody deserves some pleasure."

Faith turned to face her. "What do you expect from me? I like what you're doing here. I didn't think I would, but I do." She took a deep breath. "But it's not my calling. It's yours. And my family hasn't had money for long enough to make me prepared to tie it up in a risky investment."

Dahlia realized the pain in Faith's voice had nothing to do with the donation, and everything to do with where the money came from.

Faith's parents were *nouveau riche*. Wealthy enough to send their daughter to exclusive finishing schools, but not blue-blooded enough to be accepted by the ton. Their money didn't just come from trade—it came from volatile trade in the much-derided textiles industry.

Today, it was here. Tomorrow, it could be gone.

"I should've known this day would come," Faith muttered with a sigh.

Dahlia sat up straight. "You should've known one day you'd be lying on a chaise longue in a rundown abbey serving as shelter to homeless girls?"

"I should've known *you* would be," Faith clarified. "From the moment we first met."

Dahlia grinned. Her mother's worst memory was

one of Dahlia's favorites. The day she'd met Faith, twelve-year-old Dahlia had been lugging a bucket of food scraps out the servant's exit of Lady Upchurch's house party in Bath.

Thirteen-year-old Faith had been outside the townhouse walls, peeking into another world from the hedgerows. Not at the fine ladies and gentlemen conversing in the main parlor, but the children her own age playing battledore and shuttlecock in the rear garden.

Most of the girls attended the same finishing school as Faith did. Yet no one had invited her to the multi-day house party…even though her family lived next door.

The Digbys could *afford* to live in a fashionable address. They just didn't deserve to, according to polite society Good money came from one's ancestors, not from trade. Faith would never be mistaken for one of their own.

"You would have been lost without me that day," Dahlia informed her.

Faith grinned. "I *was* without you, after barely a minute. Your mother flew out the side door and all but dragged you off by your hair."

That was also the night that Faith had met Lord Hawkridge. Back when he was a dashing young buck on the cusp of graduating from Eton to Oxford.

But Dahlia knew better than to mention his name.

"I'm not just looking for donations," she said instead. "Or volunteer work. In your case, it really would be an investment."

Faith raised a brow. "Investing in a school that doesn't make any money?"

"I own it," Dahlia said simply. "You could, too. Agree to help me manage it, just for thirty days. If, at the end, you don't believe in the project, you can simply walk away. But if you think we're doing the right thing... I'll sign fifty percent ownership into your name and make you a full partner."

Faith sat upright. "Why would you do that?"

Because Dahlia was desperate. Because Faith was a wonderful friend. Because if there was any way at all for the school to keep itself afloat, Dahlia could finally stop stealing trifles to pay for cheese and bread.

"You would be the perfect partner," she assured her skeptical best friend. "I know you're still angry that your finishing school counted 'seaside bathing' as an educational pursuit. You hate anything that's superficial or pretentious. That is an asset. You won't let *our* school waste its students' time. I have no doubt that the two of us together can do far more good than I can do alone."

"It's not my money," Faith reminded her. "It's my father's money. I have a small allowance, not his purse strings. I may not be able to donate anything at all."

"You have your brain. That's even more valuable. With you managing the school's budget, the funds should last much longer. You can help me decide what's worth continuing and what isn't."

Faith twisted her lips, then nodded. "Thirty days?"

Dahlia sagged with relief. "Thirty days."

With luck, the two of them would figure out a permanent solution to keep the school open.

Chapter 9

When he arrived at work the following morning, Simon was unsurprised to discover he was the first inspector at the office. Dawn had yet to rise over the soot-smeared horizon. Even the fruit vendors and washerwomen had yet to take to the streets.

What Simon did not expect, however, was the threadbare woman sobbing in the rear of the center cell.

He sat at his desk. Other officers' prisoners did not concern him. Every investigator has his own assignments to attend to.

And yet.

Under a pretense of looking for some lost object, he made his way close enough to the prisoner to take her measure.

She was older than Simon. Perhaps late thirties or early forties. The gauntness to her frame indicated how long it had been since her last meal. The rouged lips, kohled eyes, and gaping bodice indicated her trade. The bruise on her left cheek indicated how badly things were going.

The Justice of the Peace must have sent about another missive commanding the officers to clear the unsavory element from the streets.

Prostitution wasn't illegal, but being "lewd" or "disorderly" was. Unless they were causing trouble, most officers left the streetwalkers be. Some, however, preferred to make an example of them. Particularly when the magistrates decided they wished to sweep the prostitutes from the streets. After being whipped or jailed, the women went right back to the only lives they had ever known.

A quick glance assured Simon that this one had been given a blanket and a tin of clean water.

One night before the turn of the century, a score of beggars and streetwalkers had been locked up without or water in roundhouse at St. Martin in the Fields in the middle of July. When officers arrived the next morning, four of the women had perished from the heat. Two more died the next day.

Simon was determined to never a miscarriage of justice like that happen again.

"Do you need anything?" he asked.

What a ridiculous question. This woman obviously needed *everything*.

"No." She wiped her face. "I have water, thank you."

He should return to his office. She wasn't his prisoner. She said she was fine. And yet logic said she wouldn't be. Gaol was often deadlier than the streets. Her constitution was already not at its healthiest.

"Have you a husband at home?" he asked.

"No," she said. "A daughter."

No father. Just a child.

He ignored the twist in his gut. Their situation was completely unlike his. For all he knew, this was a widow, who turned to prostitution only after the man who had loved her for many years had died. Or who was inventing her story whole cloth.

Somehow he doubted it.

Simon made his way back to his desk and forced himself to sort through his papers. He should be focusing on catching the Thief of Mayfair, not wallowing in memories of his childhood.

His mother hadn't been a common streetwalker. She had been a fashionable courtesan. Beautiful and charming enough to catch the eye—and the heart—of a marquess.

The marquess hadn't destroyed Simon's mother's life by ruining her or impregnating her or refusing to marry her. He'd destroyed her life by loving her.

If he would have simply left her alone, at any point in their clandestine, tumultuous relationship, she would still be alive.

For that, Simon could never forgive him.

His mother had been easy to sweet-talk. She accepted him in her bed, time and again. Accepted his money into her accounts. Encouraged Simon to do the same. Didn't he want a nice toy? Some new shoes?

He'd wanted a father.

~~A *real* father.~~

Not a savings account to buy trinkets from while his father was back home with the family that mattered. Simon was content to let that money rot in the vaults where it lay. He was his own man. And proud of the name he had made for himself.

It bloody well wasn't his father's name. It was his mother's.

Not that he was ever allowed to speak his father's name. Even when the marquess snuck them off to some countryside where he wouldn't be recognized, Simon was still to refer to him as Mr. Smith or Mr. Baker. Never "Lord Hawkridge." Never "Papa" or "Father."

That appellation was reserved for the real son. The important one. The one the marquess talked about endlessly. *Zachary is doing so well at Eton. Zachary rides better than any lad his age. Zachary will get top marks at Oxford.* The son he was proud of.

Simon had cared, for a very long time. And then he had managed to forget for a while. To live his own life. A better life. One that didn't include any Marquess of Hawkridge.

Until he'd glimpsed his half-brother at the Cloven Hoof and all those old hurts and jealousies bubbled back to the surface.

Perhaps it was a good thing Simon's father hadn't thought his mistress and by-blow were as valuable as more important people. It had achieved the result of Simon believing the exact opposite.

He withdrew a slender iron key from his pocket and made his way back to the metal bars.

No, his mother was nothing like the bedraggled streetwalker crying softly in the back of the cell. But they were both people with lives, with hopes, with children. If his mother *would* have ever found herself at the mercy of the constabulary...

Simon hoped they, too, would have had enough heart to let her go.

Chapter 10

Now that Simon knew the secret knock for the Cloven Hoof, gaining entrance to the establishment was no problem. For an officer who neither drank nor gambled, however, maintaining the cover of an average gaming hell customer required far more ingenuity.

After taking the measure of the primary salon, Simon noted that not every patron at the gaming tables actively wagered. Many simply enjoyed a glass of port or a dram of gin whilst they watched their fellow confederates turn their pockets inside out.

He was in luck. Observation was his greatest skill.

Simon procured a finger of gin at the bar, then assumed a position near enough to the tables to be reasonably assumed a spectator, yet close enough to the shadowed walls to remain out of notice.

He hadn't chosen gin because he intended to drink while on duty, but because the barmaid served little enough in the glass to have to worry about actually imbibing it. A glass of wine or a pint of ale that always brimmed to the top would be far more intriguing than just another cull nursing a glass of gin.

Today, his target was not sequestered in the rear of the club, but seated up front with a well-dressed gentleman. Simon knew that companion to be the same duke who frequently hosted masquerade parties for select members of the Beau Monde.

This was interesting, not because the masquerade parties were relevant in any way, but because the duke was now the second titled gentleman Simon had witnessed frequent the establishment.

The duke was in no way hurting for money, which led credence to the idea that the Cloven Hoof was in fact a legal gentlemen's club. Only pitiful wretches with their pockets for let were reduced to begging for credit at seedy gaming hells.

A new patron entered the pub. Simon stepped backward in dismay. What was that he had been thinking about the irresponsible sort of ne'er-do-well that would frequent an illegal gaming hell?

His half-brother, the infamously penniless Lord Hawkridge, had just walked through the door. Again. For the love of God.

Simon let out a sigh of frustration. Of course the marquess was a regular. A club like this—fine enough for the semi-fashionable, clandestine enough to rub shoulders with the rest—was the perfect environment for a marquess with a failing estate.

From time to time, Simon couldn't help but wonder what had happened to all the money.

Despite his philandering father's harsh personality, he had always kept his mistress well. Because of that, Simon had never been certain if he and his mother were cared for or simply…managed. Like horses in a rented stable. When his father didn't come round for weeks or months on end, those careless gold sovereigns had quickly begun to turn Simon's stomach. Neither his compliance nor his affection could be so easily bought.

From the day his mother had died, he had sworn never to accept another penny that had come from the marquess's pocket. But in the back of his mind, he'd always wondered what the estate might look like today, if Simon had been managing the purse strings.

After all, Simon was the first-born son. If he had only been conceived on the other side of the blanket, *Simon* would be the current marquess.

He watched from behind his glass of gin as Hawkridge joined the duke and Maxwell Gideon at the far table.

Perhaps he had been too hasty to presume that the presence of a duke signified anything at all about the legalities of the establishment. As far as Simon was concerned, being born Quality quite often meant the exact opposite.

He pulled out his pocket watch for what felt like the

hundredth time that day, and thrilled to discover it was finally half seven. His dance card was very full, starting promptly at eight o'clock this evening.

Simon set his gin where it would eventually be noticed by a thirsty patron and strode out the door.

He wasn't sure what exactly flipped his mood from somber to giddy on the short ride to the school. Possibly the wind in his hair. The joy of flying on the back of a steed. Or the knowledge that a few short minutes from now, his hands would not be wrapped around a cup of gin, but rather the far more intoxicating curves of a certain headmistress.

Their interactions could go no further than innocent dancing. An inspector's first priority was the City, and to date it had swallowed every waking hour of Simon's adult life. There was no room in his schedule for added responsibility. He had taken great pains not to make any personal connections.

And yet he was as excited to visit the St. Giles School for Girls as Prinney had been to unveil the Royal Pavilion.

His knock on the door was answered by neither Molly nor Miss Grenville, but rather a different pinafored butler with plaited hair and a snub nose.

"Good evening," he said with a bow. "I am tonight's dancing-master."

She grinned back at him as she hung his hat and overcoat on their hooks. "Can I have the first dance, Mr.

Spaulding?"

"I believe your headmistress already claimed that honor," he said sadly. "But if you are very swift after the demonstration, you might be the second on the list."

"I'll try," she promised in a whisper, then led him to the rear chamber.

As before, all of the other schoolchildren were present in the salon. This time, however, they were on their feet, with scrubbed faces and pristine pinafores and not a complaint in sight.

Upon the dais stood Miss Grenville—in an evening gown rather than trousers. Simon could not suppress a pang of disappointment. Miss Grenville would be magnificent in form-fitting buckskin.

At her side was a young lady that could almost be her twin, were it not for the shape of her cheekbones and the lack of curl in her hair.

"Mr. Spaulding," Miss Grenville called, her eyes lighting as her gaze met his. "Come. There's someone I'd like you to meet."

He bowed to both ladies. "Your sister, I expect."

"How did you guess?" asked the younger Miss Grenville with a wicked smile. "Are you some sort of sleuth?"

"The worst sort," he assured her. "Even without the family resemblance, the violin in your hand quite gave it away."

"Mr. Spaulding," Miss Grenville interrupted. "This is my sister, Miss Bryony Grenville."

"What are you going to play for us tonight?" he asked.

"Obviously a waltz," she replied without hesitation. "I have to see with my own eyes whether the two of you truly—"

"No waltzes," Miss Grenville interrupted, enunciating each word as though the subject had been broached a dozen times before. "Play a country-dance."

"Boring," Miss Bryony muttered as she lifted her instrument to her chin.

The music that poured forth from her violin was anything but boring.

Simon was struck so speechless at first that he forgot that he was supposed to be dancing. When he recalled what he was about, he swung Miss Grenville down from the dais and onto the dance floor, where they crisscrossed in lively box patterns in time to the music.

As soon as he glimpsed one of the older girls moving her feet with the rhythm, he pulled both her and the underbutler into the pattern so they could make a proper square.

Once the girls had the figures memorized, they split to form new groups of four until everyone in the salon was moving in and out of each other's paths in accordance with the melody.

Some of the older students teased each other with exaggeratedly grand movements. Some of the younger students fairly ran in place just trying to keep up with the others. But every single face in the whirling crowd was alive with excitement and laughter as their feet moved and the music soared.

Miss Grenville's eyes caught his from across the salon, and Simon realized he too was grinning like a madman. One of his dance partners was barely taller than his waist and another was too busy pulling comical faces to mind where her feet landed, but Simon hadn't had an evening more full of fun since…

Well. He could not recall the last occasion in which he had had fun.

Now that Miss Grenville was in his life, he rather suspected it would not be the last. He blinked, disconcerted at the realization that he rather enjoyed this woman turning his routine topsy-turvy. With her, he didn't have to think like an investigator. He could let their encounters play out as they would, and simply enjoy being a man.

Without breaking her gaze from his, she exchanged dance partner after dance partner until they were once again sharing the same figure.

"I thought we weren't to be seen together after we demonstrated the proper figures," he teased.

"I am Headmistress," she reminded him, eyes twinkling. "I make the rules."

Without warning, the music abruptly changed from a country-dance to a minuet.

Miss Grenville tossed a darkling look over her shoulder at her sister. The students moved back to give their headmistress and dancing-master more room.

"Oh, dear," he said with as much faux sorrow as he could muster. "It's a two-person dance. I don't suppose you've room on your card?"

She smiled up at him. "Yours is the only name that matters."

As they whirled in perfect unison about the room, he felt like the luckiest man in all the world. His mother had been right.

One should never let an opportunity to dance slip away.

Chapter 11

"*Yes*," Bryony said the moment Mr. Spaulding was gone and the children were abed. "Absolutely. I like him."

"I didn't ask," Dahlia muttered, as she poured two cups of tea.

There were no cakes or scones to go with the tea, but she couldn't have eaten anyway. Her stomach was too full of butterflies.

"He's dark and handsome and gruff," Bryony continued with a little shiver. "My three favorite qualities in a man."

"You can't have him," Dahlia snapped, before she realized that was precisely the reaction her sister had hoped to provoke.

Bryony clapped her hands in triumph. "I knew it. What are you waiting for?"

"*Everything*," Dahlia blurted. "Bryony, I'm not sleeping. I'm barely eating. I spend every moment of every day here at the school, looking after the girls, the accounts, the upkeep. I have no time for a beau. Nor can I afford the distraction. Not now. Not when the future of the school is so uncertain."

Especially not when the man in question was a Bow Street Runner and Dahlia was a thief.

Fortunately, he had no reason to suspect her. That was the beauty of being who and what she was. Her peers among *le bon ton* would never suspect one of their own. Particularly not a debutante with titled parents. And working-class men like Mr. Spaulding would never suspect a simple headmistress would be granted access to fancy places in the first place. It was the perfect ruse.

Dahlia just wished she didn't have to resort to such measures in the first place.

"I understand your passion. Honestly, I do." Bryony stirred her tea. "But while it's noble to have a passion in life, you can't let it *be* your life. No matter how worthy the cause. You are just as important as your students are."

"We're all equally important," Dahlia agreed. "But my future isn't in jeopardy. If the school fails, I can simply move back home. My days might not all be filled book clubs and high teas, but personal needs would be more than met. My students don't have that luxury. And before you preach at me that working myself to death won't help them either, I am working on a solution."

Bryony lifted her brows. "What kind of solution?"

"Financial and administrative." Dahlia rubbed at a stain in the tablecloth. "For one, Faith Digby has taken a half-partnership interest that I hope will become permanent."

"But that's wonderful!" Bryony exclaimed. "Faith is perfect. She's thoughtful and clever, and her family has more gold than Midas. All those cotton mills in Yorkshire—"

"It's not Faith's cotton," Dahlia reminded her sister with a sigh. If only it were that easy. "But perhaps her father can be convinced to donate. In any case, Faith's assistance will be invaluable."

Bryony grinned. "Particularly if she can manage your schedule to accommodate more time for Mr. Spaulding."

Dahlia rolled her eyes to show her complete dismissal of the topic and lifted her tea to her lips.

The unfortunate truth was that she was far from disinterested in the idea of spending more time with Mr. Spaulding. She had meant every word about not having the time for courtship, nor even the luxury of being able to devote her private thoughts to what could have been, had circumstances been different.

And yet her brain was ungovernable. If it decided to evoke memories of his smile instead of sums for the accounts, or to conjure the feel of his strong hand guiding the small of her back instead of letting her sleep—what was a headmistress to do?

Especially one as desperate as Dahlia.

"There will be no romance with Mr. Spaulding," she informed her sister firmly.

Bryony sighed. "Because he isn't 'one of our set.'"

Yes, but not for the reasons Bryony supposed.

Mr. Spaulding was a Bow Street Runner. Moral, ethical, honest. He believed in clear distinctions of right and wrong. He believed in law, in punishment, in justice. In letting the system dictate everyone's future.

Dahlia, on the other hand, would pilfer the Prince Regent's peaches and roasted meats right from the Carlton House royal buffet tables, if it were the only way to keep her students from starving.

She didn't need a flirtation with an officer of the court. She needed the support of people like her, who would do anything in their power—laws be damned—to save the lives of others.

If Mr. Spaulding learned of the risks she'd taken to keep bread in her students' bellies, he would stop more than his flirtations.

It wouldn't matter that the stolen baubles made their way back to their rightful owners, or that she only went to such lengths when the pantry was empty and the overdue rents couldn't be another day late. His oath to the court would require he treat her no differently than every other thief whose necks were stretched in the gallows.

As a nonpareil of moral uprightness and the sort of

good, caring man the world deserved far more of, Mr. Spaulding was a perfect model for destitute young girls who had seen little reason to have faith in men.

But as for Dahlia... She could not dare indulge feelings that would risk far more than her heart.

Chapter 12

The following morning, Simon breakfasted alone in his tidy flat on Seymour Street. In fact, in the long decade he had lived at this residence, he had only ever dined alone.

His nocturnal schedule prevented him from attending social events. The one time he'd invited his housekeeper to join him for supper, she had politely informed him that she knew her place, and it was not beside her employer at the table.

So he dined with case notes, rather than company.

Previously, it had never bothered him. His aloneness wasn't *loneliness*. It was a strategic tactic to ensure no distractions would interrupt his focus. Being personally responsible for the most challenging cases meant work was never far from his thoughts.

Some investigations not only hinged on having the presence of mind to notice unobtrusive details, but also long hours of surveillance or paperwork or any number of other time-consuming tasks.

Indeed, Simon himself barely spent any time in this apartment, save the minimum required for sleep, sustenance, and bathing.

But this morning was different. His dreams were different. He had awoken not with thoughts of edicts to sweep the streets of unsavories or the crimes of the maddening Thief of Mayfair, but rather the laughing eyes of a certain St. Giles headmistress.

What might Miss Grenville think of Simon's living quarters?

His apartment was far grander than any home her students would have ever seen, yet not situated close enough to Hyde Park Corner to be considered fashionable. Its clean, ordered interior was Spartan at best. No paintings or fluted moldings adorned the walls. While there was no butler or livery on staff, his housekeeper also served as a quite competent chef, and his footman doubled as a valet.

He was neither rich enough to be considered gentry nor poor enough to want for any comfort, making his home unremarkable in every way.

Quite the opposite of Miss Grenville.

Everything about her commanded attention. Her dark, expressive eyes, her enthusiastic gestures, her big heart. The battered abbey she had converted into a boarding school had cracks on every surface, worn edges on every corner, and yet even the most cavernous of rooms seemed filled to the rafters with life and laughter.

Trying not to think about her only worsened matters. Miss Grenville's infectious high spirits clung to him like the scent of fresh biscuits, making him smile at odd moments even when she was nowhere about.

Another man would have formally courted her by now. Another man *would* win her hand and make her his bride.

That man would not be Simon. Marriage would not negate the need for long hours in his office, at the court, on the case. Any woman naive enough to be his wife would quickly find herself alone in an empty apartment, taking meal after meal without a conversation partner, because her husband was off interviewing witnesses or jailing criminals.

He respected all women far too much to offer less of a marriage than what they deserved.

Several other men on the force felt much the same way. Whenever they found themselves yearning for female company, they merely sated their masculine urges with one of the city's countless prostitutes.

Even though he knew that tens of thousands of women—from penny whores to fashionable courtesans—relied on trading their favors for wages, Simon could not join their clientele. He had witnessed what being a kept woman did to his mother. He would not risk accidentally fathering a child. The streetwalker remedy of sponges soaked in vinegar was not always effective.

Simon was living proof.

He was unwilling to lie with any woman he wasn't proud enough to make his wife. Nor would he wish for any offspring of such a union to feel unworthy, to be an embarrassing mistake his father must lie to conceal. Someone needed to be trustworthy.

If that meant suffering along with neither mistress nor prostitutes, so be it. In the event that Simon did someday fall in love, he wished for it to be with a woman he was honored to court openly, a match he was not only willing to admit to but eager to celebrate.

Looks and familial background mattered little, so long as she shared the infallible ethics and honest nature Simon had dedicated his life to upholding.

Unbidden, his thoughts returned to Miss Grenville. She was simultaneously quite close to and very far from the image he might have conjured in his mind.

Her positive attributes were obvious and abundant. So were the rather alarming qualities that gave him pause.

She was benevolent, but outspoken. Unselfish, but impulsive. Brave enough to take a broom to the head of a miscreant, and foolish enough to have risked it. Girlish enough to curl her hair into ringlets…yet shockingly at ease in a pair of men's trousers. In short, not the unquestionably above-board proper young lady of his dreams.

And yet, were those passionate qualities not the very things that drew him to her? That enabled her not only to open a school as improbable as hers, and to have the grit and conviction to keep it going despite the odds?

Miss Grenville might not comport herself in the manner that society dictated, but that was only because of her remarkable capacity for kindness and charity, and her utter disinterest in anyone whose nose got bent out of shape over it.

He would stay on as dancing-master because, try as he might, he could not imagine cutting her from his life completely. She gave everyone light, where before there was shadow. Even a soul as hollow as Simon's.

But just as her life was dedicated to saving the girls of her school, Simon's was dedicated to protecting the rest of the City. It would be best for all parties affected if he and Miss Grenville limited their interactions only to those that best served her students.

No matter how empty his home suddenly seemed without her.

Chapter 13

"*Spaulding*," came an exasperated male voice. "Did you hear a word I've said?"

Simon glanced up from his stack of notes on the Thief of Mayfair to see a clump of his colleagues outside his office door. "I'm sorry. I was lost in a case. What did you say?"

"A few of us are heading to the races," said one of the other officers. "A new Thoroughbred is taking the Long Course, and we plan to rent a stagecoach to see it. There's room if you want to join us."

Simon put down his pen. Lately, he had become more aware that the other men kept inviting him to activities, despite his constant refusals. But how could they expect him to make the sixty-mile trek to Newmarket Heath in Suffolk, just to see a horse? He could not possibly turn his back on his cases for days on end.

"Thank you for inviting me," he said, surprising his

men as much as himself. "I'm afraid I have pressing matters here at home."

"This isn't home," one of the inspectors reminded him with a wry look. "This is work. Take care to mind the difference."

Simon inclined his head in acknowledgment. He couldn't help but wonder what expressions his men might wear, had they glimpsed him dancing the minuet with a school full of street children.

Hiding a smile, he scooped up a select few of his scattered notes and tucked them into his breast-pocket for safekeeping on the ride to Grosvenor Square. Once he reached Mayfair, he paused on the opposite side of the road as the fashionable townhouses and removed the first handwritten note.

This was the list of houses the thief had targeted, in as near to chronological order as Simon could figure. Each time the thief struck, Simon investigated a multi-street radius.

The majority of his information had not come from the victims—who were in far too much popular demand to bother making time for a Runner, especially given their missing object had been returned—but rather, from interviewing pawnbrokers around the city.

None could describe their transaction with any more clarity than "grubby" or "street urchin." By *not* being a person of importance, the client had failed to register at all. Particularly since the items themselves were not especially unique or attention-grabbing.

The pawnbrokers that agreed to speak with Simon had assured him they hadn't had the least inkling of the items' dubious origins at the time of its purchase. The prices then paid to retrieve each object were well over market value, making the entire transaction well worth the pawnbrokers' time…and their silence.

The thief was not only counting on all of the above, but Simon also believed the malefactor had devised his crime *specifically* to exploit those exact traits. How could anyone investigate a robbery that few reported, nor would bear witness to?

But the clever thief had not counted on Simon. Even a single complaint was worthy of investigation.

He nudged his horse forward down the elegant row of connected brick façades. Because he had failed to be born into the Beau Monde, Simon had never met most of the inhabitants. He knew a few names from *Debrett's* and a few faces from the caricatures, but without the list in his hand, he would be hard pressed to distinguish the owners of any given townhouse from another.

Except for one.

The Hawkridge residence was the specter of all Simon's foolish childhood dreams. Of being welcomed inside the primary residence. Given a seat at the table with all the others. Perhaps he'd be offered a kaleidoscope for his amusement, a puzzle of Europe to improve his mind, and a brother to play with.

Humbug. He had never stepped foot into any of the

grand townhouses, much less been invited to take part in anything that went on inside. Worse, he hadn't even been able to keep what little family he did have. His mother had been ripped from him far too soon.

She and the marquess had gone away on one of their many trysts. As always, his mother had entreated Simon to join them on their clandestine holiday, but by then he was no longer a child but a grown lad, angry with his father for refusing to acknowledge either of them, and frustrated with his mother for accepting it as her lot in life.

As it turned out, the Big Secret was not meant to be kept. On the way back to London, an armed highwayman robbed their carriage.

Neither of his parents survived the encounter.

To this day, Simon did not know the details of what happened. The carriage and the corpses were found the next morning. The highwayman, never. The grief was still with him.

For years, he had blamed his father for his mother's years of misery and senseless death. No man should indulge in a relationship, secret or otherwise, with a woman he was ashamed to acknowledge.

Once he had finally realized no amount of rage could alter the past, Simon turned his focus to the future. He hadn't been able to save his mother...but London was full of mothers.

Full of nearly one million people just trying to live

their lives.

He hadn't been born Quality, but he could still be important. Simon held far more pride in his Bow Street calling card than he would have held in inheriting a coronet. He had *earned* the title of Inspector. Continued earning it every day. The world could be capricious and unfair, but the law was just. All written down in black and white. With men like Simon, dedicated to upholding justice.

His shoulders straightened. He shook out his piece of paper and forced himself to concentrate on the thief plaguing Mayfair today, not the one who had robbed him of his parents years ago.

One of the passing phaetons slowed, and its expensively foppish driver tilted his carefully styled hair at Simon. "I know you from somewhere...the Cloven Hoof!"

He recognized the well-dressed dandy as the one the gamblers had called Mapleton. The prat who had boasted his winnings were enough to make actresses perform any act he wished. Charming fellow.

"Indeed." Simon forced a smile. "Mapleton, is it?"

"I knew you'd recognize me." The dandy chortled in delight. "Everyone does. I'm friends with all the important people. Nothing happens in Mayfair that I don't know about. But you're not from around here, are you?"

"I'm afraid not," Simon said flatly. "Just riding through."

Mapleton nodded. "I can tell by your horse. If you

had any money, it would be pulling a carriage. Or at least it would be a nicer horse. I have several nice grays, myself. Matched pairs. I bought them at Tattersall's. Nothing else will do, of course."

"Of course," Simon murmured, though he doubted his side of the conversation was necessary.

"Well, you must be connected enough, if you're welcome at the Cloven Hoof. Gideon is *very* discerning when it comes to his patrons. I'm sure you noticed the Duke of Lambley is often in attendance?"

Simon gathered up his reins. "I—"

"He's one of the only dukes in the club, but don't let that fool you. Some of the others are too uppity for gentlemen's clubs, like Ravenwood and the new Courteland. But *Lambley*, now that's a man who throws a fine soirée. I presume you've heard of his masquerades? I shall be getting an invitation soon, I'm certain of it."

"I have no doubt it's in the post as we speak," Simon murmured.

"Exactly so. Now that Fairfax has taken over as doorman—oh!—We're not supposed to know such things, much less talk about them. It's just that when one has the ear of everyone important, it's impossible not to overhear the latest gossip. Sometimes I wish I weren't so popular."

Simon wished his horse wasn't blocked in by the phaeton.

"At least my visage doesn't appear in the caricatures," Mapleton continued. "I'm sure you've seen all the drawings Wainwright had to endure? One might think they'd stop calling him the Lord of Pleasure now that he's wed, but just this morning I spied a sketch of him wooing his wife at the opera. I have never seen a man more in love. It's unsightly."

While he was cornered with a man who vomited gossip, Simon might as well steer the conversation back to his investigation. Perhaps this Mapleton would be useful after all.

"Would you say you're a regular at the Cloven Hoof?" he asked.

"Not just there," Mapleton gushed. "I'm a regular everywhere fashionable people can be found. Most of them will be attending my dinner party next week. I only invite the titled ones, of course. I can't wait to show off a new acquisition from my latest collection. They'll all be dreadfully jealous."

Simon's brows arched. "Aren't you concerned about the Thief of Mayfair?"

"A lesser man might be," Mapleton said with contempt. "I'm smart enough not to keep my valuables on easy display. Besides, the names who attend *my* parties have no need to steal trifles. I'm friends with dukes, viscounts, earls... I even invited the Old Dragon!"

Simon blinked. "The what?"

"Lady Pettibone, who else? The queen of the Quality. She can make or break anyone with a nod of her silver head." Mapleton gave a little shudder. "Her attendance at my soirée would make me literally as important at the Prince Regent."

"Literally," Simon echoed with a straight face.

"I would invite you, old man, now that I've let the cat out of the bag. But a party is only as exclusive as its guests, and you're clearly not titled." Mapleton waved a careless hand. "Obviously you understand why you're not welcome where the important people are."

Simon ground his teeth behind his smile. He'd understood the rigidity of class lines his entire life. This was the first time he was tempted to plant someone a facer for it.

Mapleton frowned. "And yet, I saw you at the Cloven Hoof. Very curious. Have you been a member long?"

"Not long."

Mapleton leaned back in relief. "There. You see? I knew you could not have been."

"Life would lose all meaning," Simon murmured. He kept the conversation back on topic. "When did the Cloven Hoof first open?"

"You may be surprised to learn that I honestly don't know. The two things Gideon doesn't speak about are his past, and his private life. Even to *me*," Mapleton added in obvious frustration. "I can say it's been several years, although I didn't gain my own admittance until last Season, after a particularly generous donation."

"What sort of man would you say he is?" Simon asked.

Mapleton stroked his chin in thought. "I would never gossip about a friend, especially not one as powerful as Gideon. I'd never heard of him ten years ago, and have often mused whether he's connected to the underworld. He has so many secret dealings, I wouldn't dare cross him. Yet, he can be kind when he chooses. Take Hawkridge for example."

"*Hawkridge.*" Simon's shoulders tightened.

He should have known no discussion of the Beau Monde would be complete without his half-brother being mentioned.

Mapleton nodded. "Hawkridge is the perfect example of what I mean. Everyone knows the man is all but penniless. He's no stranger to the caricatures himself. But the marquessate was ruined by the time Hawkridge inherited it. The fact that he's kept it afloat for all these years is testament to...well, *something*, I suppose."

Simon lifted his brows. It would be a remarkable feat, indeed. If it were true. He doubted it. Their father had left Simon money. A relative pittance, but still. That only proved the point. Surely riches would have been heaped upon the marquess's legitimate son.

"What do you mean, the estate was ruined?"

"That father of his." Mapleton waved a hand. "Houses, horses, whoring. It all adds up. Look how fast Prinney is spending the budget."

"Whoring?" Simon repeated, his tone lethal.

"Well, one cannot know for certain if there were whores, plural, but you cannot imagine the scandal when he died in the arms of his mistress."

"Killed," Simon said through clenched teeth. "They were murdered. By a highwayman."

"Then you do recall the story! The marquessate still had some value, but because the new Lord Hawkridge wasn't yet of age, some guardian controlled the purse strings and destroyed what little was left. The poor bastard had no choice but to marry a horse-faced heiress."

Which meant Simon's father *had* left his legitimate son money. Pots of it. He couldn't imagine what it must have been like to have to wed for money because someone *else* had frittered an entire inheritance away.

"Wait." Simon frowned. The story was off. "No, Hawkridge isn't married."

"Well, not *yet*. He's postponing the inevitable, if you ask me. Always claiming doesn't want any old horse-faced heiress. He wants to find one he *loves*." Mapleton flapped his hands to his heart in mockery. "Have you ever heard such twaddle? Gideon and the others tease him all the time. Everyone knows marriage is a business decision."

"Perhaps he has yet to come across an heiress that would do," Simon offered, then grimaced. Had he just defended his half-brother?

Mapleton snorted his contempt. "Rubbish. He's had mountains of opportunity. Or at least he did, when he was younger. With every year, the situation is more dire. The dowries that would have saved Hawkridge ten years ago won't make a spot of difference against today's debt. If you could only see the numbers on his account at his tailor's."

That sounded more like what Simon would have expected from a spoiled marquess. "He continues to incur more debt that he knows will never be paid?"

"He claims it will. Debts of honor, and all. But it's his own stubbornness getting in his way. Gideon offers to buy him a bottle of port time every time he sees him, and Hawkridge always refuses. Same old mummery about accepting credit but not charity." Mapleton shrugged. "When Hawkridge's investments do take a turn for the better, he runs about town settling everything he can. Gideon is always first."

Simon frowned. "Because Gideon is a dangerous man to owe debts to?"

Mapleton shook his head. "Because they're friends. That's what Hawkridge is like. I did invite him to my party. How could I not? It will be the feat of the year if he finds his elusive heiress under my roof. I'd be the most celebrated host of the Season!"

"I shan't keep you." Simon took this opportunity to quickly gesture toward the road. "I am certain a Town gentleman as popular as yourself has a thousand friends to attend to."

"*Lord*," Mapleton effused as he picked up his reins. "Someone like you could never imagine the burden it is to receive so many important calling cards."

Simon should have been elated to watch Mapleton's carriage disappear from view. Instead, all he could think about was the gossip about his brother.

If even half of it was true, Hawkridge wasn't responsible for destroying his father's legacy after all. Some unscrupulous guardian was.

Which meant Hawkridge was just a man postponing a loveless marriage as honorably as he knew how. He had friends. Fears. A future he couldn't control.

Simon swallowed his years of envy. His half-brother might not be the judgmental, uppity one after all.

Neither one of them had won.

Chapter 14

"Stay close to me, and mind your step as you exit the carriage," Dahlia instructed the gaggle of little girls squeezed on all sides of her in the hired coach.

Ahead of them was the hackney containing the older girls. Faith was in the coach behind theirs, overseeing the last third of the students.

"I've never been to the circus!" several of them gushed.

The truth was, none of her students had been. As it was one of Dahlia's favorite entertainments, she could think of no better way to reward them for their commendable behavior.

The problem was convincing her new administrative partner.

"How is this possibly a wise idea?" Faith groused as she wrangled her queue of schoolgirls against the outer wall of Astley's Royal Amphitheater and out of the path of the people streaming inside.

Dahlia took the youngest two girls by the hands. "I promised the students one outing per year, and it's already been eleven months with nothing. We have the cheapest tickets in the entire amphitheater, and the girls are about to have the most fun of their lives."

"No more fun until next year," Faith said firmly. "Not until our financial security improves."

Dahlia nodded. "No more fun without express permission. I promise."

"Can we go in?" the girls asked. "Is it time?"

"It's time." She grinned at her charges. "Follow me, everyone."

It was impossible to say what hit first: the roar of the crowd, the blur of bodies, the smell of sawdust, or the crackle of magic in the air. Every time she entered the amphitheater, its electric atmosphere was overwhelming. She longed to be onstage, in the ring, up in the balconies. Only by being everywhere at once would anyone have a prayer of truly experiencing everything the circus had to offer. For the first time, she would finally be able to share a small morsel of that magic with her students.

The last time Dahlia had attended the circus, she and her family had been seated in one of the expensive orchestra boxes with a ground-level view of the stage.

Today, she and two dozen schoolchildren were going to trek to the top of the four-story building, to the very back of the amphitheater, at the opposite end of the stage, where their tickets allowed them entrée to a cramped public balcony with no benches or amenities.

The girls were already in heaven.

"*He's standing on a horse,*" squealed one of the youngest ones, pointing over the edge of the balcony to the sawdust ring below.

"Have you ever seen a curtain so grand?" one of the older ones asked in amazement as she caught sight of the billowing black fabric covering the stage from floor to ceiling.

When the orchestra began, they all stopped speaking at once, awed at so many instruments and so much sound as the music filled the amphitheater. Dahlia's blood sang. Her favorite childhood memories were the evenings she and her brother would return home after the circus and practice all the tumbles until they'd worn holes in their clothing. The most disappointing moment of her young life had been the day she learned the best career she could hope for was that of "duchess" and not "tight-rope dancer."

She and Faith moved to the back of the box in order to let the girls have the best view of the ring and the stage.

"Did you look at my ledger entries?" Faith asked quietly.

Dahlia's shoulders dropped. "Yes. It was much as I feared."

Faith nodded. "We either need to spend less or raise more."

"I'm trying." Dahlia's muscles tensed. "Running the school takes almost all of my time. But now that you're here, I can go back to looking for donations."

"I'd help if I could," Faith said, her voice almost too soft to hear. But they both knew she wasn't the one with connections.

"You are helping," Dahlia said fiercely. "And your father's donation enabled us to purchase our very first materials. Now that we've chalk and blackboards, we can teach the girls to read."

Faith gave a wobbly smile. "Proper classes."

"Proper classes," Dahlia agreed. "Maids that can read would be able to follow lists made by the house-keeper. Even sent out to shop, if the kitchen needed something from market."

Faith hesitated. "Do you think anyone would hire the girls as anything but maid-of-all-work?"

"We'll make certain of it," Dahlia said in a tone that brooked no argument.

The truth was that although maid-of-all-work was grueling, twenty-hour-a-day work with minimal pay and no days off, any one of their girls would be fortunate to be offered such a position. So many other children in their position ended up in brothels or on the streets.

Unless she could teach them the skills to achieve something better.

Dahlia straightened. "When Bryony visits, she leaves the house with a different maid as chaperone each time, so the girls can interview actual staff members on what it is really like to be a chambermaid or scullery maid or lady's maid."

Faith inclined her head. "That's something. Have you also thought about more practical mathematics?"

Between acts, they bent their heads together, whispering and debating their ideas for the school. Dahlia was thrilled. She was the vision, Faith the execution.

She was so focused on creating a plan for the future that she scarcely noticed the comedians, tragedians, and contortionists in the ring below, until the curtain abruptly closed for intermission and she suddenly had two dozen excited schoolchildren all speaking to her at once.

Amid the rapturous descriptions of clowns and riding-masters, one of the girls asked, "Where is Mr. Spaulding?"

Molly looked up sharply from the back row. "You invited him, did you not? You said you would."

"A lady would not dare ask a gentleman anywhere," Dahlia said with prim disdain.

"You promised," the girls shouted. "You said he could come!"

"I did not ask," Dahlia clarified. "I begged quite appallingly. He'll meet us after work, if he's able."

The girls' cheers were cut short by the rising of the curtain, indicating intermission was over and the sights and orchestra would recommence.

"I think they like him as much as I do," Faith whispered with a smile.

"Please don't tell me your favorite rogues are the handsome gruff ones," Dahlia muttered.

Faith burst out laughing. "That sounds like something your sister would say."

"She's incorrigible," Dahlia agreed with a shake of her head. "Bryony thinks our compatibility on the dance floor indicates our bodies are destined for a waltz of an entirely different sort."

"How intriguing," rumbled a deep, familiar voice from right behind her. "How may I be of service?"

Heat flamed up Dahlia's neck and flushed her cheeks as she turned to face the very gentleman she'd been having decidedly impure thoughts about. "*Mr. Spaulding*. I... That is..."

He lifted her fingers to his lips, promptly robbing her of any further ability to think.

Never before had he touched her outside of dancing. She had appreciated the cautious distance between them. His precise adherence to the professionalism of his duties as a Bow Street Runner. The formality he took care to uphold during his weekly role as dancing-master to schoolgirls.

For the past few weeks, he had carefully kept their attraction in check; their limitations, defined. It only made him all the more tempting. It had not been easy for her to continue to ignore their obvious attraction. Here, it would be impossible.

The expertly tailored tailcoat encasing his wide

shoulders and muscled arms was not the deep, distinctive blue of his usual greatcoat, but a soft dove-gray that brought out the summery blue of his eyes. Her pulse jumped.

Mr. Spaulding was not here in his capacity as a Bow Street Runner, or to serve as dancing-master to the distracted children peering over the balcony at the sights below.

Tonight, he was here for *her*.

He exchanged half-shouted greetings with Faith over the cacophony of the music and rambunctious audience, then returned to Dahlia's side. She hoped he never left. He was the one man whose electric presence held more restrained power than the entire circus.

"I wasn't certain you would be able to come," she said.

"Nor was I." His blue eyes held hers. "But I am glad I did."

"Do you like the acrobats?" she asked.

"I am fascinated," he responded. But his eyes were focused on her, not the performers below.

If they were in a ballroom, Dahlia would know just what to say, precisely how to act. She would flirt with her eyes above a painted fan, perhaps whisper something shocking into his ear whilst they waltzed beneath the chandeliers.

But they were not in a ballroom. She had no painted fan, no dancing slippers, no excuse to be in his arms. Mr.

Spaulding was not one of the practiced rakes or self-important dandies who cluttered the teeming rooms at Almack's and made every dinner party seem the same as the last.

With him, she never quite knew what to expect. Every time she'd thought she had figured him out, she had been wrong.

The night of their first meeting, she had not expected to see him again. He had returned, despite all expectations. Just like he'd said he would. He'd brought crumpets, stood in as dancing-master, attended the circus.

Had he done so solely because he wished to help her girls? Or was it in part because he, too, looked for any excuse to share a single moment together? Her pulse fluttered.

"Do you attend the circus often?" he asked.

She shook her head. "I did when I was younger."

"I bet you imagined yourself the riding-master atop a rearing stallion," he said with a smile.

"A horseman?" she said in mock affront. "You don't see me as a confectioner of costumes, or perhaps as one of the dancing girls?"

"You could never be relegated to the background," he said softly. "I can't look anywhere else once you've entered a room. You were born to be the star of the show."

Her heart pounded. "Perhaps it's not me, but your

eyes that have the problem."

"Problem?" he echoed in surprise. "There's no-where else I'd rather look."

He held her gaze for an extra heartbeat, then glanced down at the ring below.

She wished he hadn't. Now it was she who could not look away, and she no longer had the excuse of conversation to hide her absorption.

He was more handsome and wild than any of the stallions below. Confident. Strong. Tamed...barely. Every time she was with him, she couldn't help but suspect his buttoned-up exterior hid unbridled passion beneath. Especially when she caught him staring at her with a heat that stole her breath—and her inhibitions. When he looked at her like that, she longed to rip his buttons away one by one until he was forced to do something about it. Something that involved her mouth on his and their hands on bare skin.

Dahlia swallowed. She had to put a stop to this mad attraction.

He stood shoulder to shoulder with her, facing the circus, yet she suspected that, just like her, his attention was not on the antics below, but rather on the proximity of their bodies. Close enough to touch. Wise enough not to.

Yet her skin tingled with the electric knowledge that were she to—*ahem*—accidentally succumb to a swoon, she would fall directly into his embrace.

Such thoughts were beyond dangerous. She could

not allow their connection to be anything other than completely professional at all times. Her school couldn't afford such folly.

Dahlia had already lost significant status by becoming a headmistress in the first place. She needed every social tie she still possessed in order to keep the donations flowing and the school afloat.

If she were to marry "beneath" her—or, worse, have a passionate love affair with a Bow Street Runner—she would ruin far more than her reputation. She would lose all funding for the school, and destroy her students' best chance of surviving the rookeries.

No matter how much she longed for his kiss, she could not allow him that far into her life...or her bed.

Chapter 15

Even before the circus came to a close, Simon discovered himself desperate to prolong the evening. He had assumed a four-level amphitheater filled with frenzied music, flying sawdust, and raucous applause would be the one place in which his attention would be drawn to something other than Miss Grenville's magnetic presence.

He had been wrong.

His blood did not rush because of the tightrope walkers or the horses prancing backwards on two legs, but rather due to the proximity of Miss Grenville's infectious smile and laughing eyes. He enjoyed the circus because *she* enjoyed it, and he loved watching her reactions.

When she clapped in glee, or gasped in shock, or whispered to her delighted charges that she would *love* to find room for acrobatics in the school curriculum, every word, every smile, softened the stiff edges of armor he'd spent two-and-thirty years building around his heart.

He was in very, very deep trouble.

"Thank you for coming," she said, her eyes still sparkling with excitement. "We know how busy you must be, and are thrilled you could share this moment with us."

Simon wished he knew whether she truly spoke on behalf of her students…or for herself.

"I cannot recall the last time I shared such a charming evening," he said truthfully. "Please allow me to accompany you all to your carriages."

"Oh, you don't have to do that," she demurred. "We haven't any carriages, and must hire hackneys."

Of course he had to. Especially now that he knew they would be standing alone in the dark and the cold, waiting on hacks with enough space for all the children.

"It will be my pleasure," he said, and offered her his arm.

She grinned up at him as she curved her fingers about his arm. "You are a true gentleman, Mr. Spaulding."

He was nothing of the sort. But he made no reply. Her hand on his arm had quite robbed him of speech. He was pleased that she thought of him as a gentleman, however figuratively. He would strive to ensure she always thought of him highly.

Many years ago, when he had first realized the

chasm between high society lords and accidental off-spring, he had embarked on a dogged mission to prove himself equally as worthy of the title of "gentleman" as his brother.

Destined to failure. No gutter-class turnip could compete with the sons of dukes, earls, viscounts. They had Oxford and Cambridge. He had a ripped sack of discarded library books. They had lofty titles. Simon's was *bastard*. They had family money and limitless con-nections. His had consisted of a courtesan who counted every penny.

It had never been a fair fight.

His mother had chided him for the one-sided com-petition with his brother. Why should Simon care about people who didn't even know he existed? A gentleman in deed was a gentleman indeed, and the only society that mattered were the people one chose to keep close to their hearts.

Foolish claptrap. Of course the opinions of others mattered. England's entire society was powered by the infallible opinions of strangers. Prinney, the House of Lords, even the patronesses of Almack's—*those* were the voices who were heard. They were the important ones. Not by-blows like Simon.

But those were the words of a mother who loved her son. Despite himself, Simon had started to believe. He was able to push his brother if not out of his mind completely, then at least out of his day-to-day thoughts.

Eventually, he no longer wished to pretend to be

part of that world. He now had status in his own. A career. A purpose.

And, if he was lucky, perhaps could even have a good woman. After all, Simon didn't need to be like the self-important society toffs. If he were, he wouldn't be here with Miss Grenville. He couldn't stop glancing at her from the corner of his eye.

She was so different than other women of his acquaintance. So *present*. He couldn't imagine losing her or the thousand-and-one shared moments at the school. When he was near her, she didn't let him be an impartial observer on the fringes. She made him take part. Made him *be* part.

Despite every well-worn shield he possessed, she had slipped into his world and made him care.

"This way, if you please." He herded her troupe to one of the least crowded exit queues, then held open the door to count heads as they walked by.

At least they had missed the rain. The headmistresses' two umbrellas would provide little protection from a downpour. Simon squinted into the wind. The sky was too dark to judge whether the danger was truly past, but for now the scattered puddles were clear of ripples.

When Miss Grenville, Miss Digby, and twenty-four schoolgirls were safely out of the amphitheater, he led them past the row of fine carriages awaiting their owners to the rear of the line of coaches, where those hoping to hire a ride waved down potential hackneys.

"Let me guess," Miss Grenville said, her eyes teasing. "You came on your horse."

"I did indeed," Simon admitted gruffly. It was the fastest way to get to her.

For the first time in ages, he wished he did own a carriage. One large enough to fit a fair number of her students…and cozy enough to raise no eyebrows if he and Miss Grenville were forced to sit side by side.

Even then it wouldn't be enough.

He slanted a glance at her. The rim of her bonnet hid her face from view, but that did not stop his heart from pounding. They suited in so many surprising ways. He could not wait to learn more about her. But he wanted to do it right.

As an investigator, he had unequal power to probe into people's lives. After he joined the force, he realized snooping into other people's unrelated affairs to appease his personal curiosity was more than unethical.

Invading their privacy would make him little better than the thieves who stole property without permission.

As his career wore on, his casework grew so quickly he wouldn't have time for idle sleuthing when there was so many active cases that required his complete attention. The past few months had been especially full. Too full. His moments with Dahlia had been the only respite.

He would let their relationship unfold at its own pace. There was no need to rush her or himself. He was having *fun* for the first time in ages. A little bit of mystery was probably good for him. It made his chemistry with Dahlia completely unlike any other encounters he'd ever had. More magical.

Now that they were outside and stationary, there was no reason to keep her hand locked about his arm. Yet he made no move to let go.

Neither did she.

She tilted her face toward his. "Are you ready for dance lessons on Saturday?"

That brief hour had quickly become his favorite moment of every week. He feigned a look of deception. "I thought I heard you say we would now have acrobatic lessons instead of dance classes."

"You're not ready for acrobatic lessons." She patted his arm consolingly, her eyes laughing. "Stick with what you're good at."

He did his best to look offended. "I believe you managed to both compliment and insult me in the same breath."

"I have many talents," she promised with a wicked smile. "Insulting handsome gentlemen isn't even my best one."

"Tell me more about these hidden talents," he demanded, leaning his head a little closer.

She trailed her fingers from his forearm up to his bicep. "Well, for one thing…"

"A hack!" Miss Digby yelled, waving madly as a lumbering, patched-up carriage slowed to a stop. "Over

here, children! Youngest ones first. Same groups as before, please."

Although Simon had not been present at the time of
their arrival, he doubted the mad dash of mud-splattered
boots toward the dry interior of the hackney cab at all
resembled the orderly procession Miss Digby was hoping for.

"Not your turn!" shouted one of the younger girls
as she pushed an older student out of the way—and directly into an oversized mud puddle.

Simon leaped toward her even as she was falling, but
was still too far to be able to save her from splashing
backward into the puddle.

He scooped her off the ground and upright the moment he reached her side, but it was too late. She was
soaked from head to toe. Her sodden dress clung to her
thin legs as embarrassed tears slid down mud-splattered
cheeks.

"Are you all right?" he asked.

"I'm fine." Her chin jutted upward defiantly. "She's
just a baby. I'm older. Can take the next hack."

Brave words that clearly did little to help her save
face amongst her peers, now that her threadbare pelisse
and carefully styled hair were bedraggled with muddy
water. The wind only made matters worse, adding an insidious chill to the cold, damp air.

She wrapped her wet arms about her torso and
ducked her head to hide the chattering of her teeth.

Simon's fingers were already at the buttons of his

tailcoat before he stopped to think what he was doing. A gentleman never exposed his shirtsleeves. Not in public, and definitely not in view of ~~thousands~~ hundreds of witnesses.

Such depraved indecency would be considered scandalous, at best. And he had finally gotten Miss Grenville to think of him not as a Bow Street Runner or even a dance instructor, but as a man. A *gentle*man. A perilously thin façade.

But whatever a gentleman did or did not do, Simon Spaulding had no intention of allowing a ten-year-old girl to catch the ague when he had a perfectly warm, perfectly dry tailcoat to drape about her shoulders.

He shucked off his coat in haste. His starched, bleached sleeves billowed in the wind as he wrapped his coat about the girl's wet, trembling frame. If gooseflesh rippled up his arms from the knifelike breeze, this child must have been chilled to the bone.

"Is that better?" he asked quietly.

She nodded, her eyes shimmering. "Thank you."

Boots slapped against wet earth as Miss Grenville skidded up beside him. "Louisa, are you all right? Is anything bleeding?"

"I'm fine." Louisa swallowed visibly. "Please don't punish her. I didn't listen to Miss Digby. Punish me instead."

"I think you've both been punished enough," Miss Grenville said softly. "If you're strong enough to queue with the others, a second hack has just arrived."

"I'm strong," Louisa said, shivering. "Ain't cold at all. Thank you for letting me stay."

Before Miss Grenville could speak another word, Louisa wrapped her arms about her ribs and raced to join the others.

"Your punishments must be terrifying," Simon murmured.

"Not mine. Her father's." Miss Grenville let out a deep breath. "Half the girls in the school expect a whip or a cane every time something goes wrong. No matter how much love I give them, it'll be a long while before they stop expecting to be tossed out on their ears."

Simon's heart hurt for them. "And now you've given them a home. It must feel like a miracle."

"Perhaps to them." Miss Grenville's gaze softened as she watched her students file into the second hack. "But I'm no angel. And none of this is easy."

Simon had no doubt it wasn't easy. It was harder to believe that Miss Grenville wasn't an angel. "You're doing an impressive job."

Her grateful eyes snapped to his. "You're the impressive one. You had Louisa warm and safe faster than I could run."

"Keeping people safe is my job," he muttered, feeling ridiculous in his straw-colored waistcoat and flapping shirtsleeves. "I'm no hero."

"Tell that to Louisa. She'll probably never take your coat off. That was probably the first time in her life that a gentleman was ever kind to her."

"A gentleman would never allow his toilette to be in such disarray," he said wryly.

"Then I don't want a gentleman." Miss Grenville's eyes held his. "I want you. Just as you are."

I want you. Warmth filled him, and Simon was suddenly impervious to the chill of the harsh wind.

Miss Grenville was obviously referring to his interactions with her students, but a growing part of him hoped he might suit in more ways than one.

As he handed her into the third and final hack, he couldn't help but wonder what it might be like to see her every day, rather than once a week. To say good night while she was still in his arms.

He wasn't ready to allow the thought of something as permanent as *marriage* to complicate his unfalteringly simple life, but nor did the idea of things returning to how they were before he met Miss Grenville hold any charm.

Long ago, he'd stopped asking himself where he was going, what he wanted, because he believed he'd already achieved it. For more than a decade, he'd worked from sundown to sunrise close to seven days a week. He had a good job. He was one of the best inspectors on the force. What else could he want?

As Miss Grenville's hackney trundled away, the answer was suddenly clear.

He didn't want to be stuck in the past anymore. He

wanted a new future.

One that included Miss Grenville.

Chapter 16

After three maddening days trying to get Mr. Spaulding out of her thoughts, Dahlia gave up in defeat and set out for her parents' townhouse. Perhaps what she needed wasn't to push her fantasies from her mind, but rather to talk the situation through with the most brutally honest of all her siblings.

Except Bryony was not at home. Nor was Heath. Or Cam. In fact, the only family member currently present in the Grenville family home was Lady Grenville herself.

Which was how Dahlia found herself perched on the edge of an overstuffed sofa, sharing one of her mother's infamously awkward teas.

"I don't know how you can claim feathers to be *boring*," Mother was saying now. "The right ostrich feather can make all the difference in whether one's bonnet is *en vogue* or *outré*. Look at yours, if you don't believe me."

"What's wrong with mine?"

"It hasn't even got a feather," Mother spluttered. "That's what's wrong with it. And the top is all wilty, as if it had been left out in the rain."

Dahlia pointed to the windows. "It's raining."

"One's bonnet needn't show it, darling. You've an umbrella, do you not? Surely you didn't sell it to raise money for your little school."

"What a lovely idea, Mother. Thank you for thinking of it."

"Don't you dare sell that perfectly nice umbrella. The pearl trim cost two months of your pin money, as I recall. Quite the cleverest purchase I'd ever seen you make."

"I was sixteen. It was probably the first purchase I ever made. By selling it, I could buy cheaper umbrellas for every girl in my school."

Or shoes. Or books. Or paper. Or globes. Anything to fill the empty schoolroom.

"Cheap umbrellas!" Her mother flapped a hand. "How I wish you wouldn't bicker so. It is a challenge to stay levelheaded in the presence of someone determined to thwart logic at every turn."

"It is indeed," Dahlia muttered as she helped herself to a second lemon tart. "Will it help if I promise never to carry a cheap umbrella in your presence?"

"It would help if you gave up that school altogether."

"Mother—"

"I know we've been over this already. I know. But

you are the daughter of a baroness."

"Being a headmistress doesn't make me less your daughter."

"It makes you *seem* less," Mother warned. "If you won't give up the school, at least be conscious of how you present yourself. Your Almack's voucher will be the least thing you'll have lost, if you go too far."

"I'll lose access to tepid ratafia and dancing with outspoken roués?" Dahlia asked dryly.

"You'll lose soirées altogether," Mother said sharply. "And house parties, and balls, and dinners, and teas. Can you think of anything worse?"

Dahlia could, in fact, think of hundreds of worse tragedies. However, her mother's arrow struck truer than she might have thought. Losing her last ties with society would be an unmitigated disaster. The last thing Dahlia wanted was to alienate the very people she hoped would help support her cause.

She set down her tea plate. "You're right. I would not wish for that to happen."

"I'm always right." Mother beamed at her. "And I have very good news. Despite your unfortunate activities as of late, I have managed to wrangle invitations for both of us on Sunday night."

"Invitations where? To meet a duke? An earl?"

Mother's smile faltered. "I'm afraid even I have been unable to return your name to those lists. But have no

fear, darling. There are a half dozen others who will accept you. We shall flit to them all as if we haven't a care
in the world. I suspect Lady Upchurch will have those
lemon cakes you adore."

Dahlia had known taking a role as headmistress
would inherently make her less fashionable, but she
hadn't realized her philanthropy with the school had
sunk her status so low as to make even low-quality invitations difficult to obtain. Her stomach went cold at the
thought.

Her ambivalence at being "a baroness's daughter"
had been nothing more than bravado. She might not
have appreciated the constant reminder, but in the back
of her mind she had always counted on it.

The entire reason she'd been brave enough—or, it
seemed, foolish enough—to found a school like hers in
the first place was because she'd assumed she would always have access to some percentage of the ton's
pocketbooks. There were always ladies looking for a
good charity to sponsor, and as Dahlia was a lady herself,
the financial aspect had seemed easy.

Except it had never been easy, and was getting
harder by the day. She now had Faith on board to share
the administrative load, but that was only half the battle.
Faith hadn't been able to rub shoulders with Dahlia's circle, even before she'd agreed to be joint headmistress.

If Dahlia lost that advantage too, what would that
leave them?

"All right," she said. "I'll go to the party."

"More than one?" Mother asked hopefully.

"All of them." Dahlia rolled back her shoulders. She would go, she would *flit* as her mother said, and she would work back into the ton's good graces. It was the only way.

"Darling, that's marvelous!" Mother clasped her hands together in excitement. "You may even find a husband. Bring the right man up to scratch, and you'll never have to fear being cut from society again."

Dahlia didn't have time for a husband. Not to be the arm bauble of some marquess or viscount. Until she had the school sorted, she didn't even have time for Mr. Spaulding. She had to focus on the big picture before she could fritter time on herself. The girls' futures depended on her.

"I'll go," she repeated. "But I'm not husband-hunting. I mean it, Mother."

"You're not getting any younger, darling. A new crop of young ladies make their curtsey every year."

"Let them. I have my own group of girls to worry about."

"You and that school!" Mother slammed down her teacup. "That's enough unladylike pursuits. You need to grow up, give up, and get married. While you still can."

The flicker of anger that flashed through Dahlia was aimed not at her mother, but society in general. Who decided that five-and-twenty was too old to find a husband? Or that becoming headmistress of a philan-thropic school meant she no longer even deserved one?

Perhaps her mother was right, and she was on a path that would lead her far from everything she'd ever known. If one couldn't bend the road, then one would simply have to bend the rules. Not being able to stay in both worlds didn't mean there wasn't a compromise that would allow her to keep a foot in each.

After all, her primary responsibility was to whom? Herself? Her school? The law? Society manners?

None of that. Her number one priority hadn't changed from the time she was a child. The thing she cared about most had always been and would always be her family.

Which now included twenty-four orphan and runa-way girls, as well as two sisters, one brother, an absentee father, and a smothering, overprotective, well-meaning mother.

She couldn't bear to lose *any* of them. And yet it felt like it was happening.

"Once a week," she said. "I'll go to parties with you once a week."

Mother gasped in delight. "And you'll let me match-make? I'll offer you only the very best, I promise."

Somehow, Dahlia doubted she and her mother shared the same taste.

"I'll be cordial to everyone you introduce me to," she allowed. "As long as you stay calm when I invite the other ladies to donate to the school."

Mother leaned forward to grasp her hands. "You're a good daughter, darling. I just know there's a man out there who won't mind your foibles."

Dahlia managed to smile without clenching her teeth. "Thank you, Mother. That's very heartening. I can hardly wait to become an insipid society wife to someone whose title matters more than I do."

"Oh, wouldn't that be lovely?" Mother sighed happily. "What if all three of my daughters captured the hearts of lords!"

"My heart is aquiver at the very idea," Dahlia assured her.

It was not.

Yet the thought of marrying a man with money was undeniably one of her mother's better ideas.

Not a lord, to be sure. Being a duchess or countess or marchioness carried far too many responsibilities to allow any time for overseeing a charity boarding school. Nor would any man of nobility or pretensions to it allow her to continue.

Through the rest of the tea and all through the carriage ride back to her school, Dahlia couldn't quit the idea from her mind. Marrying someone she didn't love had never held much appeal to her, but what if doing so solved all the rest of her troubles?

Her mother would be thrilled to have yet another daughter safely wed. If the gentleman in question were rich enough not to care how or where his new wife spent his money, was it selfish of her not to at least try?

She doubted any of the eligible dandies in her mother's social circle could ever hold a candle to the flame Mr. Spaulding was capable of igniting with a mere glance in her direction, but she wasn't looking for passion. Her girls needed stability. Marriage was simply a business decision.

Everyone in the ton knew that.

She stepped out of the carriage and made her way to the front door, intending to march straight up to her office to take a cold hard look at her finances…and her future.

As soon as she unlocked the front door, however, she overheard the telltale sound of muffled sobs coming from the stairwell.

"It's not fair," came the voice of little Beatrice, one of the youngest girls. She had been left on a workhouse doorstep as a baby, and at seven years old had the oldest eyes of anyone Dahlia had ever seen. "Louisa, you don't understand."

Dahlia hesitated in the middle of the entryway. She hated to hear one of her girls cry. Yet interrupting might cause more harm than good. She bit her lip and decided to give the girls a few more moments.

"You're wrong," Louisa said. "About everything. You *do* have a mother."

"I'm an orphan. And if I'm not, then I might as well be," Beatrice said brokenly. "My own mother didn't love me enough to keep me."

"Yes she does," Louisa insisted. "That's not your mother. Headmistress is. She's leagues better than an ordinary mother. Headmistress would *never* give one of us up."

Dahlia's heart caught. She pressed a hand to her throat and closed her eyes.

"Headmistress is my mother?" Beatrice asked in wonder.

"She is now," Louisa said firmly. "Look around at all our sisters, Bea. We'll never be alone again. We have more family than anyone else in all of London!"

A long silence stretched out through the stairwell before Beatrice said softly, "We're the luckiest girls alive."

Dahlia sagged against the foyer wall, her throat too clogged to swallow. If Louisa and Beatrice were the luckiest girls alive, then Dahlia was, too.

They were right. This was a family. As their surrogate mother, Dahlia would dedicate her life to the school, not to herself. She'd find a way to keep this their home for as long as they needed it.

No matter what it took.

Chapter 17

For Dahlia, the most unreal part of executing a double flip off a supper sideboard onto the school's dancing rug wasn't the men's trousers covering her legs or the squeals of her students as she flew through the air, but the fact that she had an audience at all.

Other than with her sisters—and her brother Heath, who had taught her acrobatics for lack of anyone else to play with—her facility with contortion and fearlessness to taking flight had always been a well-kept secret. If her parents had ever suspected their children of practicing the tumbling feats they witnessed at the circus, they would have ceased the family outings altogether and likely forbade Heath and Dahlia from being in the same room.

When Heath grew of age, he was able to join Gentleman Jackson's, and practice fisticuffs with all the other fashionable gentlemen.

For Dahlia, there was no such outlet. Without her brother, she could only tumble alone, which was both less fun and less safe than their previous teamwork.

It was the one moment in her otherwise unremarkable life when excitement raced through her veins and every nerve came alive. Colors were brighter, sounds sharper, her reflexes lightning fast.

For years, tumbling had always been her favorite pastime. Her truest self. And, above all, her most guarded secret.

Until now.

She couldn't let anyone outside of her school know of her activities. But here, inside these walls, she and her girls would be free to be themselves.

"Today's class is not about acrobatics," Faith called over the noisy cheers.

The students booed good-naturedly.

"That's right." Dahlia drew herself up in the center of the room and clapped her hands for attention. "Today's tumbling class is about two things: exercise, and self-defense. If it goes well, we'll do it weekly. Especially during inclement weather."

"I hope it always rains!" shouted a girl in the back to loud laughter.

"Next lesson in self-defense," Dahlia announced. "Always be aware of your surroundings. Are there people? Slippery surfaces? Sharp edges?"

"You was in the Army?" one of the students called

out.

"Worse," Dahlia answered. "I have a brother."

The girls erupted in giggles.

"The reason we want to know who else is within shouting distance," Dahlia continued, "is because the best way to win a fight is not to get in one at all. If help is near, or someone who could go find help, that is always the first step. With luck, it's the only step needed to a peaceful resolution."

"What if nobody else is near?" called out one of the girls.

"What if there's lots, and all of them are bad people?" called another.

Dahlia nodded. "That's why you're paying attention to sharp edges and slippery surfaces."

"So you can push them?"

"Precisely. And so you don't hurt yourself. In many situations, our biggest enemy is ourselves. When you panic, you lose logic. You can't think. You only react. That's why you have to be aware of your situation well before panic sets in."

"But how?"

"You train yourself to pay attention. Your brain can learn to do it automatically." Dahlia took a step back. "Everyone, close your eyes."

"Miss Digby's eyes aren't closed," called a voice.

"Neither are yours!"

"Everyone means everyone. Ready?" Dahlia grinned at Faith. "Without opening your eyes, name the slippery surfaces inside this room."

"The center carpet?"

"The wood, when we wax it."

"Top of the sideboard!"

"Not for Headmistress."

Dahlia clapped her hands. "Open your eyes. Did you miss anything? If you can't call for help, your next goal is running away. Without tripping over branches or slipping on pebbles or falling against a sharp surface."

"What if you can't run away?" called a student.

"What if he catches you first?" called another.

Dahlia knew that "he" meant someone different for every one of them. It was her hope to save her students from finding themselves in those situations again.

"Step three," she said. "Twisting out of an unwanted grasp. Miss Digby and I have been practicing. Let us see if I can escape her grip."

Given that Dahlia had been escaping her elder brother's best holds for nearly fifteen years, Faith would have little chance of keeping Dahlia trapped. But the self-defense segments before the tumbling classes weren't about standing still—it was about breaking away.

More than that, it was about giving hope to twenty-four little girls. All the lessons in the world wouldn't enable them to overpower a man twice their size. Their attacker would know that. He'd be counting on intimidation to do most of the subduing.

What the girls had was the element of surprise. Their

attacker might anticipate a tug on the wrist, a feeble kick to the leg. Tears. What he wouldn't be expecting were the moves Dahlia was about to teach her girls today. All they needed was a single second's surprise or weakness to break free and run for help. She would give them every advantage she could.

"Form a circle, and pay close attention," she called. "I'm going to show you several different options. First you'll practice with each other, and then every one of you is going to try to escape *me*. Ready?"

"Ready!" The girls scrambled into a circle around Dahlia and Faith.

By the time the hour-long exercise class was over, two hours had passed in a flash. The girls were sweaty and excited and energized. Some were better than others already.

But all of them now had hope.

"*Baths*," Faith called out. "Two lines, come with me."

Dahlia sagged against the sideboard as the girls filed out of the room after Faith.

Dahlia's exhaustion was emotional, rather than physical. She had spent more time watching and coaching the girls than feigning being an attacker, but keeping her eyes on twenty-four students at once was an impossible task. Twenty-four students who considered her their family. Twenty-four children who counted on her to keep them safe.

She wouldn't always be there, looking over their

shoulders. Maybe the school would outlive Dahlia, and maybe it wouldn't last more than a few years. Either way, at some point the girls would strike out on their own. They would be old enough to find work. Homes of their own.

Perhaps even fall in love.

A knock sounded on the front door.

Dahlia waited a second, until she realized all the girls were off having baths. There was no one to answer the door. Not that she could do it herself—not in trousers and her brother's old shirt, anyway. This time, her dress was upstairs in her wardrobe.

The knock sounded again.

With a sigh, she pushed away from the sideboard and jogged to the locked front door.

"Who is it?" she asked, doing her best to disguise her voice.

The caller paused, then said, "Miss Grenville?"

Mr. Spaulding. Dahlia ran a hand through her tousled hair, then grimaced when she recalled that was the least of her concerns. If he'd been shocked to briefly spy her in trousers before their first dancing class, he'd fall into a dead swoon if he saw her like this.

"If this is a bad time," he began.

"*No,*" she blurted. She didn't want him to leave. She just... "Are you alone?"

"Yes, why?"

She unlocked the door, jerked him in by the wrist,

and slammed the door shut behind him. "If you'd been in my class, you would have been able to break free of my grip."

"Why would I want…" His eyes darkened as he took in her form-fitting outfit. "What are you wearing?"

"The latest fashion," she assured him. "I just failed to check whether the invoice said 'gentlemen' or 'ladies.'"

He frowned at the too-long hems. "You purchased these garments?"

"I borrowed them." She sighed and cleared her throat. "Permanently."

A muscle tightened in his jaw. "From a lover?"

Dahlia stared at him, secretly overjoyed at the possessive, highly improper question. Mr. Spaulding wasn't shocked or appalled at catching her in men's clothing. He was *jealous*.

"Why do you ask?" she asked lightly, touching her fingers to the front of his waistcoat. He caught her wrists. She didn't try to break free.

"You must tell me if there's someone else," he growled.

She lifted her lashes and let him see the truth in her eyes. "How could there be anyone else?"

He pulled her arms about his neck and covered her mouth with his.

After a lifetime dreaming of her first kiss, Dahlia had spent the last several weeks praying it would be with Mr. Spaulding. He did not disappoint.

His lips were as firm as she had imagined, his mouth as hot and demanding. Every inch of his body seemed tightly coiled. Being pressed up against such a breathtaking package of hard, solid muscle made Dahlia feel all the more soft and feminine.

Her knees were weak, it was true, but the real reason she held fast about his neck was because the last thing she wanted was for him to let go. A kiss like this wasn't to be dispatched with swiftly, but rather to be enjoyed. *Savored.*

Every brush of his lips, every lick of his tongue against hers, sent shivers of pleasure along her skin and made her clutch him all the tighter. Her heart beat wildly, each frantic pulse in her breath pressing her closer and closer to him.

This was no longer a kiss.

This was a claiming.

A taking.

What was unclear was whether either of them were winning the battle. It felt like they both were drowning, melding into each other until nothing existed but the thunder of their heartbeats and the hunger in their kisses. Her thoughts were no longer her own, her body less so.

This was how virgins got despoiled. At this point, it was practically her idea. Now that she had sampled a taste of heaven, she no longer wished to settle for mere kisses. She wanted to feel his hands not spanning the many layers of muslin hiding her curves, but rather touching her bare skin. She wanted to know every inch of him.

"Miss Grenville," he murmured between kisses each hungrier than the last. "We shouldn't."

Of course they shouldn't. That was part of what tasted so intoxicating.

"Dahlia," she whispered as she nibbled the edge of his lip. "I believe you know me well enough to call me Dahlia, Mr. Spaulding."

"Simon," he growled, capturing her mouth with his so she couldn't keep talking.

But everything she wished to say, she was telling him with her body. Her fingers gripping his hair, her gasps against his jaw, her hips pressed to his—all of it was an eloquent conversation that bore no need for words.

He had no need to *ask* if she wanted him. To wonder whether it would be all right with her if he ripped her trousers from her body and taught her the advantages of being a woman. If he didn't start soon, she might begin ripping fabric herself.

"We cannot," he panted as he tore his mouth from hers.

Before she could do more than clutch her hands to her thundering chest, he spun toward the door and strode out into the night.

Chapter 18

There was nowhere Simon wished to be less than a shadowy table in the back of the Cloven Hoof.

He was far from convinced there was any mystery to be solved. Like as not, Lady Pettibone had sent him on a wild goose chase that was wasting Simon's time and the Crown's money. But she hadn't earned the hushed moniker "the old dragon" because she was a pushover. The Justice of the Peace had made it perfectly clear: the case wasn't over until Simon definitively proved Maxwell Gideon's guilt or innocence.

"In what, exactly?" Simon had asked.

The Justice of the Peace had simply sent him on his way.

So there he was in the back of a gentlemen's club that was simultaneously both more and less exclusive than Brooks's and Boodle's. Here, the yardstick of a man's worth was not his money or his title, but rather whether the club owner felt you worthy enough to be entrusted with the secret knock.

The alternative method of entry being learning the knock from someone already accepted into the club.

None of that was illegal. There wasn't even a ledger listing member names. Either you knew the knock, or you didn't. And if you knew the knock when you shouldn't… well, Gideon had placed hired muscle at the door for a reason.

That *might* be illegal. Depending on how Vigo the doorman chose to resolve conflicts.

Thus far, however, Gideon seemed to keep a remarkably amicable club. Gamblers were allowed to wager as much and as often as they wished. Drinkers were allowed to run as obscenely long a tab as they pleased. Any fights resulted in immediate eviction of all parties involved, with the instigator banned for life. Even the betting book was no more outrageous than the one the fashionable set kept at White's.

The most obvious question wasn't whether Gideon was making money illegally, but whether the man was making any at all. Which, Simon had to admit, was in itself suspicious.

Perhaps Lady Pettibone was right.

He crossed his arms and leaned back into the shadows to watch the night unfold.

While his eyes focused on the dark, candlelit scene before him, however, part of his mind was not present in the Cloven Hoof at all, but rather replaying the most sensuous moments of his recent interactions with Miss Grenville.

Her fingers touching the muscles of his arm, sliding up the front of his chest. His hands cupping her face, sinking into her hair. The victory of finally kissing her. The rush of bliss when she kissed him back. The moment she'd bade him call her Dahlia.

Dahlia. A delicate flower. An undeniably strong woman. Yet the name fit perfectly. Both were vivid, multifaceted, extraordinary.

And if Simon had not been sent on tonight's mission, he might have been kissing her lips right now.

As viscerally as missing their weekly dance lesson disappointed, his responsibilities as an inspector would always take top priority. One man missing a dance or a supper or a few hours of sleep was a small price to pay for keeping London as safe and lawful as possible. If his childhood had taught him anything, it was that criminals must be apprehended and punished for their crimes at all costs. It was the only chance to keep order in a chaotic world.

His eyes flicked to the front of the club as the doorman cracked open the door to allow in another patron. Simon let out a sigh at the sight of dark-haired, penniless Lord Hawkridge.

Simon's titled half-brother. Naturally. The night had only wanted this.

He remained in the shadows as the marquess entered, declined a drink from the barmaid, and joined a clump of dandies who were cheering on a trio of pink-cheeked gentlemen casting entire fortunes onto a wine-stained hazard table.

Why was Lord Hawkridge watching wastrels risk the rest of their lives on a toss of the dice? Did he wish he had the blunt to join, or a purse to lose? Or did his inscrutable expression hide contempt for his fellow spendthrifts, and their eagerness to flirt with a misfortune that mirrored his own?

Simon could not guess at the answers. He had never even spoken to his brother. Their social spheres were too distant, and the marquess didn't even know a half-brother existed.

He did, however, have years of observation to draw from. His jealousy of his brother's better life had made it impossible to look away as his younger brother received top marks first at Eton, then Oxford. Simon had consoled himself with the knowledge that Zachary's professors were praising his title, not his performance. The supposed only child of a marquess would not have spent grueling years hunched over ancient, water-damaged books trying to teach himself mathematics and grammar without aid of a tutor.

Simon's discovery that he had a natural ability for memorization and logic had changed the course of his life.

Zachary's life, on the other hand, had only ever had

a single course. He was born heir to a marquessate. The end.

There were no decisions to be made, no exams to study, no Justice of the Peace with the power of promoting or sacking his officers at will. Zachary was born to be Lord Hawkridge someday, and now that he'd inherited the title, he would remain marquess for the rest of his life. What care had he for numbers or hard work?

Except perhaps that long-held narrative wasn't true after all. If the marquessate was already destitute when he became the new lord, then Hawkridge clearly wasn't half bad at figures. He was impoverished, but not beggared. He would have to wed an heiress, rather than find a love match, but had managed to postpone that unhappy day thus far. In fact, an impartial observer might conclude that having a fair head for figures was something both brothers had in common.

The corner of Simon's mouth twitched. Once upon a time, he would have been horrified to think he shared any talent with his younger half-sibling. As an adult, however, Simon was oddly almost proud of him. He couldn't help but wonder what Hawkridge might think of Simon if he suddenly learned he had a brother.

Well, no sense wondering, was there? Simon was here. Hawkridge was here.

A dark, possibly illegal gambling den was perhaps not the most ideal locale to spring a surprise sibling on a chap, but since a marquess and a Bow Street employee

were unlikely to run into each other in the House of
Lords or at a private ball, the Cloven Hoof was likely the
best opportunity they would ever get.

Simon had always been a fan of taking action. Sure,
he had done his fair share of sulking over life's relentless
unfairness as a lad, but he'd simultaneously made a new
plan and worked his arse off until he achieved it. That
mixture of resolve, determination, and fearlessness
served him well in his career, speeding him up the ranks
with each impossible caper solved, every dangerous
criminal apprehended.

After so many years of charging into frays and con-
fronting armed malefactors, approaching a weaponless
stranger in a public room ought to be child's play.

And yet, *"Good day! Funny story: I'm your half-brother,"*
would be the hardest words to get off his tongue.

No matter how angry Simon had been at his father
for siring a son he was too ashamed to recognize, one of
his favorite childhood fantasies had been somehow
meeting Zachary, and becoming secret best friends.
Their father would not approve, but since Simon was
already nobody and Zachary was already the heir, what
punishment could the marquess truly bring?

In Simon's daydreams, the bond of brotherhood
easily trumped the tyranny of fatherhood. He and his
brother would ride horses together, study Latin together,
hunt foxes together, play bowls and nine pins together,
even fall in love at the same time, and promise their children would spend plenty of time together as cousins. He

had been convinced it could happen...if only Hawkridge knew of his existence.

Not only had the opportunity for those boyhood fantasies long passed, so had both of Simon's parents. Even if he did introduce himself to his brother, what proof did he have that his claims were true?

The most likely outcome was not that the two men would ride stallions off into the sunset on some brotherly adventure, but rather that Hawkridge would laugh in Simon's face, turn his back, and immediately put him out of his mind.

Worse than rejected. Dismissed as insignificant.

As Simon watched, Lord Hawkridge stepped away from the hazard game to glance at the corner table he often shared with the club owner, Maxwell Gideon.

The table was still empty. It had been empty all evening. Either Gideon was not in attendance tonight, or he was holed up in his private office at the back of the club. There was only one way to know for certain.

Apparently following the same train of logic, Hawkridge craned his neck toward the passageway leading to the back office. The hallway was empty. Even the private tables were empty, save for a lone gentleman in a dark corner, blurring with the shadows. Hawkridge would have no inkling that the stranger was an inspector, or his half-brother. As far as the marquess was concerned, Simon was nobody at all.

Unless Simon changed his mind.

With visible annoyance, Hawkridge cast another frustrated glance at the vacant side table, then stalked through the smoky gaming room toward the back of the club.

This was it. If Simon wished, he could remain part of the woodwork, and let his brother pass by without a word, or even meeting his eyes.

Simon rose to his feet.

"Hawkridge." The word came out gruff. Scratchier than he would have wished. But at least it was spoken.

The marquess's answering glare would have frosted a lesser man. "I'm late."

"You're not late," Simon corrected, irritated at his brother's casual rudeness to a total stranger. "Gideon's late. You've been waiting. You can wait here." He gestured at an empty seat at his table.

Hawkridge ignored the invitation. "I don't know you."

Simon nodded. Fair enough. "Allow me to introduce myself. My name is Simon Spaulding, and I—"

"I know who you *are*," Hawkridge snapped. "I don't know *you* and I don't wish to."

Simon frowned. His cover was clearly not as good as he'd thought. "You know that I'm a Bow—"

"I know you're my father's by-blow. Bully for you. I'm busy." Hawkridge let out an exaggerated sigh. "Now will you step out of my way?"

"You...know?" Simon stammered in disbelief, his mind spinning. "How do you know?"

Hawkridge's laugh was as humorless as breaking glass. "How wouldn't I know? Every time he missed my birthday, my mother's birthday, my graduations, it was because he was off debasing himself with a mistress he cared more about than his own family. *Simon* taught himself geometry without aid of a tutor. *Simon* doesn't talk back to when he's scolded. *Simon* is more of a naturally born gentleman than you are."

"He...what?" Simon's voice was almost too faint for even himself to hear.

"You think you're better than me?" Hawkridge continued, his angry words coming faster. "I'm not surprised. You can't help it. You've always had it easier."

"I...*what?*" Simon spluttered. Was the marquess a madman? "You are a lord. I'm just—"

"*Free,*" Hawkridge interjected vehemently. "You've no entailed properties tied about your neck. You can do as you please, be what you please, make friends with people of your own choosing. You can even fall in love with whomever you want. You've probably already done so. Is there a Mrs. Spaulding?"

"Er..." Simon's cheeks heated despite himself. He had always believed in waiting for the right woman or not marrying at all. "She's not—"

"Well, she should be, whoever she is. Unless you're not as bright as I was led to believe." Hawkridge curled his lip as if disgusted by Simon's bachelorhood. "Honestly, if I had half the advantages you possess—"

"You had our father," Simon burst out, unable to take the selfish tirade anymore. "He acknowledged you. He *chose* you. You have his name, his home, his title."

"Bully for me, then. I've a title. Huzzah." Hawkridge shrugged his perfectly tailored shoulders. "I suppose that's my cross to bear. Now if you don't mind, I informed you that I am very busy—"

"Godspeed, by all means. I've never been happier to send a self-important prig on his way." Simon stepped out of the passageway with an exaggerated sweep of his arm. "Believe me, I shan't be bothering you again."

"Then at least that's one good thing to happen today." Hawkridge stalked past him toward the rear office.

Blood boiling, Simon strode out of the Cloven Hoof without a backward glance at his brother. He would never make the mistake of reaching out to family ever again. Simon had never had a brother before. He didn't need one now. Especially not a selfish ingrate like that.

He leapt onto his horse and charged aimlessly through the streets of London.

At least, he meant to charge aimlessly. Somehow, his horse had found its way through town to the St. Giles School for Girls.

As he tied his horse to a post, Simon forced his nerves to settle. There was nothing he wanted more than to have a calm, private moment with Dahlia, and neither she nor her students deserved to bear the brunt of his current ill humor. He wasn't at the Cloven Hoof anymore.

Within these walls, he could be happy.

He rolled back his shoulders and gave the knocker a loud rap.

When Dahlia answered the door, he nearly sagged in relief. "You're here."

"Where else would I be?" She blinked at him in confusion. "It's nearly midnight."

Midnight. Of course it was. And he'd banged on the front door. He stiffened in embarrassment.

"My apologies. Time…got away from me. I—Perhaps I'll call again tomorrow."

"Now is a good time." She pulled the door open wider. "I'm not in my nightrail yet and the girls are asleep. Come in. How do you feel about lukewarm tea?"

"My favorite kind," he said gruffly, and stepped inside.

She led him to the dining table, where a teapot, a novel, and a waning candle clumped in one corner.

He sat on the other side. "You were relaxing. I've interrupted."

"You're my favorite interruption." She placed a worn teacup and saucer onto the table and lifted the pot. "This is the third time we've used these leaves, so don't be alarmed if there's little taste or color left."

Her words were matter-of-fact. Recycling tea leaves was commonplace for those who couldn't afford fresh. And yet, the fact that she'd felt obligated to explain herself made him wonder once again what sort of life she had lived before becoming headmistress of this school.

Whatever led her down this path, he was glad of it. She was changing the destines of dozens of young ladies. Many of whom would have ended up in brothels or worse situations, were it not for this opportunity.

Simon couldn't help but wonder how different his mother's life might have been if there would have been a school like this available to her. Would she still have become a courtesan? An unhappy mistress to a married lord? Or might she have become a governess, a cook, a housekeeper, some less vulnerable position where she might have met someone who loved her enough to marry her?

Rather than drink his tea, he found himself spilling the entire story. How his father had treated his mother. How Simon had been born insignificant and had worked his entire life to be the opposite. How his fashionable, powerful, titled half-brother somehow felt *he* was the party more deserving of pity.

He curled his fists in frustration. "The tables would be turned if my father had made a different decision. If he'd done the ethical thing and married my mother, *I* would be marquess."

Dahlia curved her slender fingers over his fists.

"No, you wouldn't," she said softly. "He could never marry your mother. If he had done the ethical thing, he would have left her alone...and you would never have been born."

Simon stared at her.

She was right. *If Father had married Mummy* was a child's fantasy. Lords didn't wed courtesans. They couldn't. One of the biggest scandals of the past century was when the Prince of Wales had illegally wed his mistress, and even *he* had been forced to give her up.

Simon's father was not a gothic villain. Nor was his mother an innocent victim. If anything, their relationship had been more honest than either of them had a right to expect.

"He should not have carried on two lives," he said stubbornly. "It's black and white."

Dahlia's eyes flashed. "Nothing is black and white. The world is full of gray. All we can do is the best that we can, which often means compromising something we'd rather not. Many people have two lives."

"I do not," Simon pointed out. "Hiding one's true self is a form of cowardice."

"Spoken like someone who has never had to," Dahlia said sharply. "For many, it means survival. You cannot judge the entire world based on your interactions with one man."

"Not just him," Simon muttered. "My half-brother is a complete prig like all his titled peers, and we'll continue to be strangers the rest of our lives."

Dahlia frowned. "Does he have to be?"

He shrugged. "He wants to be."

"But does he *have* to be?" she repeated. "Might he not be pushing you away for the same reason you took so long to approach him?"

"Afraid his bastard half-brother would reject him?" Simon asked in disbelief.

"But you did," she pointed out. "He didn't have time for you today, and you excised him from the rest of your life."

"He was rude." Simon's jaw set. "He doesn't wish to be brotherly with me."

"He doesn't wish it right now," she agreed. "But things change. You've already missed out on each other's company for half your lives. Are you going to waste the next few decades, too?"

He narrowed his eyes. "Do you do this to all your students?"

She blinked back at him innocently. "Do what?"

"Force reason and empathy upon them until they become better people," he muttered with exaggerated sullenness.

"I hope so. I think that's what a headmistress *is*." She grinned. "You're an inspector. What did you detect about your brother, apart from his heinous manners?"

Simon thought back. His brother had come into the club for a purpose. He'd been expecting to speak with the owner, and for some reason that hadn't happened. He had seemed on his way to confront Gideon when Simon had interrupted.

"Hawkridge was in a foul temper before we'd exchanged a single word," he admitted. "He said the first thing that had gone right for him today was me leaving."

"Then even if his words were true, his primary frustration was targeted at whatever was going on before you clashed." She touched the side of his face. "I think you should try again."

"I'll consider it," Simon allowed, after a brief pause. "But not today."

"Not today," she agreed, and rose to her feet. "Aren't you going to kiss me goodbye?"

Simon leapt out of his chair in surprise. "Am I leaving?"

"I hope not." She wrapped her fingers about the lapels of his greatcoat. "I just wanted an excuse for you to kiss me."

"How's this for an excuse," he said as he lowered his mouth to hers. "I love kissing you."

She wrapped her arms about his neck. "Then don't stop."

Stopping was the last thing he wanted. Now or ever.

Her kisses were not the shy, tentative pecks of a maiden unsure about her suitor. Dahlia's kisses spilled forth with the same passionate abandon she met life with. Her mouth was sweet and sinful. Her tongue more than willing. She made no attempt to hide the unevenness in her breath or the heat in her eyes, but rather gave herself over to it completely.

How could he possibly resist?

No matter how hard Simon tried to push her from his mind, to maintain some semblance of decorum and distance between them, it was no use. Every breath he took carried the scent of her hair, every beat of his heart recalled the feel of her soft bosom pressed tight to his chest.

Kissing her wasn't something he chose to do. It was as natural and as compulsive as breathing. Lifting his lips from hers for even a second caused a sense of loss and longing so profound that he was helpless to do anything but kiss her again. Longer. Deeper. To imprint himself on her soul the way she had branded herself on his.

Passion such as theirs was as dangerous as it was addictive. If he were not careful, he would find himself tumbling over the precipice. And if she were not careful... He might never let her go.

Breathless, he forced himself to break the spell of their kiss.

"It's late," he said roughly. "I should let you get some sleep."

"Sleep is the furthest thing from my mind," she replied, her dark eyes luminous as they gazed up at him.

Sleep was also the last thing on Simon's mind. But, however much he loved her kisses and was eager to discover where they might lead, he refused to commit the same sins as his father. He respected Dahlia too much to make love to her without the protection of marriage. Nor would he engage in any behavior that could accidentally sire a child.

As much as it pained him to leave her, he pressed a

kiss to her forehead and turned for the door. To his surprise, he had begun to wonder whether he ought to reconsider his thoughts on courtship. The idea was as much intriguing as terrifying. There was no reason to rush things. Simon straightened his shoulders as he stepped out into the night.

He would be the first man in his family to choose the right woman and treat her as a gentleman should. Dahlia was worth it.

Chapter 19

By time she and her mother were announced at their fourth Sunday evening soirée, Dahlia's cheeks were sore from the effort of keeping up a constantly smiling façade. She was here to raise funds for her school—and her mother was here to interest eligible gentlemen to her daughter. Both goals were easier to achieve with a cheerful disposition.

And both of them were failing miserably.

The stream of insipid gentlemen her mother forced into Dahlia's path did little to arouse her passion. Too flawless on the outside, too empty on the inside. Padded tailoring to feign musculature, boots without a single scratch, pale cheeks that saw a razor more often than they saw the sun, cravats that must have required the entirety of the afternoon to fold into multilayered starched confection.

Nothing at all like Simon.

His imperfections were what Dahlia appreciated most. He had no need for padded shoulders or false calves. Her skin heated in remembrance.

A shadowed jaw meant he dropped by after work because he was thinking about her, not because he'd spent an idle afternoon obsessed with the size of his cravat. And if his boots were dusty, it was because he'd ridden hell for leather to see her.

This time, her smile was genuine. It always was when she thought about Simon.

Her mother would swoon to discover her daughter had a fancy for a working-class gentleman. Like as not, her parents wouldn't consider Simon a gentleman at all. He had no title. No father. No carriage. He had a *profession*—the horror!

But her parents would be wrong. Even now, after learning the story of Simon's birth, Dahlia could not think less of him simply for being born on the wrong side of the blanket.

To be sure, he would never fit into society. But that would be true no matter who his mother might've married. High society was high society. Working class was not. And orphan girls who lived on the streets… Well. They weren't faring too well tonight, either.

"You Grenvilles had so much potential." Lady Pettibone stared down her nose at Dahlia with the signature hellish disdain that had earned her the *Old Dragon* nickname among those reckless enough to whisper about a duke's sister behind her back. "Why on earth wouldn't you sponsor a school for young ladies more worthy of our attention?"

Dahlia ground her teeth. The question was not for her, but for the giggling social climbers who wouldn't have a thought in their heads if Lady Pettibone hadn't put it there first. The old dragon knew full well why Dahlia's school was worthy of merit. She simply enjoyed using her wealth and influence to destroy those around her.

So far, only a handful of women had agreed to spare a few pounds out of the following month's pin money to support a noble cause like Dahlia's. Any help was wonderful. Every farthing counted. But it wasn't enough.

With a sinking heart, Dahlia realized she *would* have to attend these weekly whirlwinds with her mother for the rest of her life if she wished to have a prayer of keeping her school afloat. Which meant maintaining her precarious position in society at all costs.

"Why, Miss Grenville," came a low, familiar voice. "Did I hear you've opened a boarding school?"

Dahlia's jaw tightened as she turned to face Lord Hawkridge. He had lost her good favor years ago, when he had hurt Faith Digby. Dahlia had to witness enough injustices in the world. She would not abide poor treatment of her best friend.

Now that she knew the handsome marquess was secretly the ill-mannered younger brother of her favorite

Bow Street Runner, she liked Hawkridge's company even less. Yet she could not cut him. Both slights had been confessed to her in secret.

Even if Hawkridge would have caused offense to Dahlia directly, he was still a marquess—and thus a very eligible bachelor. With the slightest murmur of disapproval from his lips, Dahlia's invitations to all future society functions would disappear in a heartbeat. No marriage-minded mama would risk alienating a titled lord in want of a bride due to having the "wrong element" on the guest list.

She would simply have to play the game.

"I did indeed open a charitable school," she answered with an ingratiating flutter of her eyelashes. "I don't suppose you'd like to contribute to the cause?"

His smile faltered.

Dahlia tried hide her pleasure that her barb had struck true. Of course he couldn't contribute. Hawkridge was at this party for a similar reason to her own. He needed to drum up an heiress to refill his family coffers.

By phrasing her question as to whether he'd *like* to contribute, she had placed him in an even tighter spot. If he said no, he'd be a heartless cad. And if he said yes, he'd have to explain why it was that he could not. A perfect question that no reputation-minded gentleman could possibly answer.

Hawkridge's only recourse would be to feign catching a glimpse of an old friend across the room, and beg his leave before the conversation could go any further.

Precisely what Dahlia wanted.

His eyes met hers.

"I *would* like to," he said quietly. "Current circumstances do not allow me to make an immediate gift, but please trust that the moment my resources improve, your boarding school will be the first and greatest recipient of any funds I can spare."

Dahlia's throat grew thick. Blast Hawkridge's self-effacing sincerity. No wonder Faith still held a *tendre* for the man after twelve long years.

"Thank you," she said grudgingly. "You are all that is generous and kind."

What she really wished to ask was where the devil his kind, generous spirit had been when his brother had displayed the courage to introduce himself.

She hadn't told Simon that she had known Hawkridge since the day of her come-out eight years earlier. The way Simon felt about people living double lives, she hadn't wanted to admit there was more to hers than met the eyes, too.

If Simon found out she was of the same social ilk as his brother, one of two things would happen. He would walk away in disgust over the subterfuge—or he would realize their class differences were too great to overcome, and cease his attentions altogether.

Either way, she would lose him. She hoped to put

off that day for as long as she could. Their romance had always been doomed. The best she could aspire for was enjoying their stolen moments to the fullest while she still had him.

"Out of curiosity, you haven't seen Miss Di…" Hawkridge coughed into his gloved fist and shifted his weight.

Dahlia narrowed her eyes. "Have I seen who?"

"No one. Nothing," he said quickly, with only the slightest flush to give lie to his words. "I am monopolizing too much of your time. Please excuse me."

Wind nearly blew from his heels, so swift was his exit.

Had he almost asked her about *Faith?* Dahlia stared after the fleeing marquess with a mix of disbelief and joy. *"No one."* Ha! She could not have devised a worse punishment.

If the *tendre* was mutual, that meant Hawkridge wanted Faith and couldn't have her. A perfect reversal of the situation in their youth.

Good. He deserved it. Even if Faith did not.

Dahlia wished she could tell her best friend about the conversation that had just transpired. But she had promised years ago not only that she wouldn't interfere in the private matters between Faith and Hawkridge, but also swore never to mention Faith's name to him, or report anything he might have said. To do so simply hurt Faith too much.

If Hawkridge wished to patch their past differences, she had said firmly the last time Dahlia dared broach the topic, then he knew where to find her. And if he did not, then Faith was much better off without him crossing her mind.

"Is he going to pay you a call?" squealed a hushed voice from behind Dahlia's shoulder.

"Mother, *no*." Dahlia turned to face her in exasperation. "I'm not interested in Hawkridge and he's not interested in me."

"How can you think that?" Mother whispered with obvious delight. "He spoke to you completely on his own, without a single subtle hint from my lips."

Dahlia could only imagine how not-subtly her mother had been prodded eligible bachelors all evening.

"I am not interested," she repeated. "I'm surprised *you* are. You must know he's penniless."

"I know he's a marquess," Mother replied primly. "I certainly wouldn't be ashamed if my second daughter became a marchioness."

"What if I just became a Mrs.?" Dahlia asked. "Or a perfectly happy old maid?"

Mother blanched. "Don't even say such horrid things. There's still plenty of time for you to find a promising match."

"Is there?" Dahlia asked. "I'm five-and-twenty. Some would say I'm *already* an old maid."

"This may well be your last viable season," her mother admitted. "That is why we must make it count.

If you are to be a mere 'Mrs.,' then by God, it will be with the finest gentleman I can beg you an introduction to. I want you to be happy, darling."

Dahlia's smile softened. She and her mother rarely saw eye-to-eye, but through the years, she had never doubted that she was loved. "I think we've exhausted the supply of single men at this gathering. Should we not be flitting to the next?"

Mother's expression brightened. "Almost. You've not yet spoken to the host of this soirée. Go bid well wishes to Mr. Mapleton, and we can be on our way. Unless he invites you for a romantic stroll in the back garden."

Dahlia valiantly refrained from gagging. Phineas Mapleton was her least favorite acquaintance of the entire Beau Monde. She would rather throw herself from Blackfriars Bridge than spend a moment alone with him. But if thanking him for tonight's party meant she could leave it all the sooner, then there was no choice but to face him and have done.

Girding her loins against what was certain to be an infuriating encounter, she rolled back her shoulders and strode toward the refreshment table where Mapleton was currently regaling a group of young dandies with one of his interminable stories.

"—which is how I began to collect globes!" Mapleton was saying, his voice rising with obvious merriment.

"All the poor bastard had to say was that he had the finest collection in all of London, and I was determined to have the largest set in England. I have big globes, small globes, colored globes, black and white globes, free standing globes, globes that spin…"

Did the man even *know* anything about globes other than their size and color? It was all Dahlia could do not to bury her face in secondhand embarrassment.

If her girls had access to even a single globe, Dahlia had no doubt they would dedicate themselves to memorizing every sea and landmass represented on its surface.

For months, she had been looking for secondhand globes in pawnshops. He had probably purchased all of those, too.

Science was wasted on a fool like Mapleton.

"When he found out I had two copies of the very pocket globe he'd been searching for," Mapleton continued with a laugh, "he had the nerve to ask me to sell him one of mine. The fool! The only reason I *found* the globe is because he was looking for it. Naturally, I bought them all. The last thing I'd do is sell one to *him*. It's not *my* duty to increase someone else's collection, is it?"

"You could give one to charity," Dahlia found herself blurting.

"Charity!" Mapleton chortled. "Now, *that's* a good laugh. If I wouldn't sell one for profit, why on earth would I give any away?"

"You said there were duplicates," she insisted, ignoring the wide-eyed faces of her host's sycophants. "If you've already multiple copies, surely you wouldn't notice the loss."

"Of course I wouldn't *notice*." Mapleton stared at her as if she were mad. "I don't even like globes. I never look at them at all. They're in boxes in one of my guest chambers." He paused to cast a *can you believe this?* glance to his friends. "As a woman, you naturally wouldn't understand. How can I make it clearer? The point of a collection isn't to have one of everything, it's to have the *most* of everything."

Dahlia didn't bother to hide the fury in her voice. "Thank you very much for that elucidating explanation. I am certain I shall have to ruminate over your wisdom for many hours before my female brain can fully comprehend the masculine joy of collecting something one isn't intelligent enough to value, just to ensure it doesn't fall into the hands of someone who might appreciate it."

Mapleton blinked, then shrugged. "There, you see? You worry about hems and bonnets, and leave the collecting to men like me."

Dahlia's answering smile was sharp enough to break glass.

But now, she had a plan.

Up until this moment, she had only pilfered small items of value out of desperation. When there wasn't enough food to fill her girls' stomachs, or the debt collectors were pointing out that debtor's gaol offered prison cells for ladies.

After that exchange, however, she wouldn't feel the slightest hint of remorse if a few of Mapleton's pocket globes were mysteriously diverted to an impoverished schoolroom in the heart of the St. Giles rookery.

The only question was how.

Chapter 20

After her mother dropped Dahlia off at the school in the family coach—and sent the driver as a guard to ensure she made it safely from the street to the door—Dahlia sprinted up the abbey steps to her bedchamber and flung open her wardrobe doors.

It was nearly three in the morning. Mapleton's dinner party guests would have long returned home, or set out in search of better parties. Mapleton himself wouldn't be able to resist dropping in to every other ongoing soirée, just to casually mention how much better his had been. His staff would either be abed, or concentrated on the ground floor, where the party had been.

In other words, there would never be a better time to strike than right now.

She exchanged her evening gown for one of the threadbare day dresses she wore when doing menial tasks about the old abbey. In case one of the servants caught her poking about, she needed to look like one of them—not Robin Hood in ringlets. She yanked the combs from her hair and fashioned a messy bun to stuff inside a mobcap. A white apron completed the outfit. Perfect.

A glance in the looking-glass indicated she appeared perhaps a little too clean to be an overworked maid at the end of a long day, but tossing soot from the fireplace onto her cheeks and gown would only cause more questions than answers. If anyone enquired, she would simply have to act like a *lazy* maid.

While her mother had been busy giving heartfelt goodbyes to her friends in the queue of partygoers awaiting their carriages, Dahlia had managed to slip a shilling to one of the milling hack drivers, and extract a promise to follow her family coach to the school.

She tiptoed back downstairs and cracked the front door to glance outside. Good. He was still there.

The hack driver believed he was collecting one of Dahlia's maids, who had been given a holiday to visit a sister who worked at another domicile. It had been the best story Dahlia could come up with. All the same, she wouldn't have him drop her off too close to Mapleton's townhouse.

She grabbed a small sack of rags earmarked for the morrow's laundry and rushed outside to climb into the hack.

"Where to, miss?" asked the driver.

Careful to keep her cap low enough to hide her face,

she murmured an address a short walk from where she needed to go.

Her attempt at an accent likely wouldn't earn her front billing at the Royal Theater, but it was good enough not to raise the hack driver's eyebrows. In no time, the cab rolled to a stop exactly where she had intended.

Doubt didn't set in until she neared the rear staff entrance to Mapleton's townhouse.

Her previous petty crimes had been far easier to execute, requiring no subterfuge at all. She simply walked a little too close to a certain shelf or table, and slipped a trinket into her reticule without anyone being the wiser.

If she would have been caught entering or exiting a chamber where she didn't belong, absolutely nothing would have happened. No one would ever imagine the daughter of a baroness to be stealing from her peers. A ratafia-laced giggle of "Where *did* the retiring room go?" and she would be sent fondly on her way.

This time would be different. She wasn't pilfering a palm-sized object in the midst of a chaotic party. She was sneaking in.

With determination, she marched up the unlit path to the servants' entrance and pulled the brass handle.

Locked. *Blast.*

She stood frozen for a few moments. What was she supposed to do now? She couldn't walk in the front door. Even if she'd worn trousers instead of a dress, she wouldn't scale the trellis to an open window. Not because she wasn't capable of such acrobatics, but because too much could go wrong if she were caught.

It was done. Her attempt to outfit the schoolroom with tools the girls could actually use was over before it could begin. Mapleton would keep the globe collection he didn't care enough about to even look at, and the schoolroom would stay empty, just as is it was before.

The door swung open.

Dahlia jerked backward so fast, she nearly dropped the sack of rags.

A bleary-eyed scullery maid with a dishrag tossed over one shoulder stared back at her.

"Er…" Dahlia pointed vaguely at the sack in her arms, her heart pounding. "I have…"

The maid rolled her eyes and stepped out of the way. "You're late. Way past curfew. All you upstairs maids are the same. Think your day starts with the sun instead of at midnight like the rest of us."

Dahlia gave an apologetic smile and rushed inside before the chamber maid could change her mind.

"Go on, then." The maid tilted her head toward a servant staircase. "If I got to work, you have to, too."

Dahlia nodded quickly and dashed up the dark stairwell. Halfway up, she sagged against the wall and gasped. She closed her eyes and tried to calm her racing heart.

As terrified as she'd been, the truth was that her infiltration had gone far more smoothly than she would ever have guessed.

Had she been a perfectly acceptable debutante attempting to enter Almack's assembly rooms without a voucher, she would have been interrogated and vetted within an inch of her life, and still denied entry to those vaunted dance halls.

As a maid, however, she'd been able to walk right through a servant entrance without so much as raising an eyebrow. Invisible, even to her supposed equals. She took a deep breath and climbed up the rest of the stairs to the second floor.

Twin rows of doors lined both sides of the empty passageway.

Behind one of those doors was the guest room with the boxes of globes. Behind another door was Phineas Mapleton's bedchamber. Possibly with him in it. Dahlia gulped.

"Lost?" came a brassy voice from right behind her.

Dahlia spun around in surprise.

"Oh, leave 'er alone, Helen. Can't you see she's a new one?" said a world-weary chambermaid to a slightly younger copy of herself. Family, Dahlia imagined.

"Course she's new," Helen said with a roll of her eyes. "Pretty maids never last for more than a few weeks. Where were you sent to clean, honey?"

"I-I'm to straighten the guest chamber with piles of boxes," Dahlia stammered in haste. "I've forgotten where it is. Can you point me in the right direction?"

Helen pointed a finger. "First door on the left."

Dahlia nodded her thanks and slipped into the guest room. A row of wooden crates lined one wall. A somewhat ominous four-poster bed stood on the other side.

She would have to be fast. The last thing she wanted was for Mapleton to catch her now.

Heart pounding, she rummaged through each crate until she found one with a dozen Newton pocket celestial and terrestrial globes. They weren't whatever rare vintage Mapleton had been referring to, but were rather the sturdy, serviceable variety like the pair she and her siblings had shared in their nursery growing up. Two sets ought to do.

Quickly, she wrapped the four smallest globes in rags and stuffed them into the small sack. They barely fit, but at least it was not obvious what they were. Time was running out. She shoved an ornate pen knife from the desk down the side of the sack before hurrying to peek out a crack in the chamber door.

No maids. No Mapleton.

With a deep breath, she raced across the hallway to the stairs and flew down the dark steps as swiftly and as silently as she could. When she reached the bottom, she didn't pause to check if the scullery maid was back in the kitchen, but rather sprinted out the back door and into the night as fast as her legs would carry her.

By the time she was able to wave down a passing hackney, she was blocks away from fashionable Mayfair townhouses. She climbed up and sagged into the worn squab. Dahlia hugged the sack of pocket globes and soiled rags to her chest, not sure if she should laugh or cry. For better or for worse, now she really *was* Robin Hood with ringlets.

And there was no going back.

Chapter 21

"Care to join us for a pint?" one of the day officers asked Simon as he walked through the front doors of the Magistrates' Court.

Simon gave him a pointed frown. "I've just started my shift."

"You're not starting your shift," pointed out one of the others. "You've worked ten nights in a row. This is supposed to be your day off. How come you never join us?"

"I don't drink," Simon said simply. "And I'm not a member of any clubs."

He certainly wouldn't be counting the Cloven Hoof.

"You don't have to drink," put in Mr. Webb, his secretary. "Public houses also have hot meals."

True. Simon glanced into faces of the other men. A few had clearly only invited him out of habit, not because they expected him to suddenly become sociable. Others, like Mr. Webb, stared back at him hopefully. Earnestly. The corner of his mouth curved.

"All right," he said. "One hour. The kitchen had better rival the prince's."

Mr. Webb's face erupted into a wide grin.

"Prinney adores overcooked pigeon," he assured Simon. "You'll ask yourself how you managed to stay away for this long."

Simon laughed, and allowed his men to lead him to a tavern not far from Bow Street. A roaring fireplace and loud, convivial chatter enveloped them in warmth the moment they stepped inside. Simon followed as his colleagues headed straight for one of the few long wooden tables not crowded with other patrons.

"Welcome to the family," one of the day inspectors said with a smile as he tilted back on his chair's rear legs.

"Enter at your own risk," said one of the others. "We fight like brothers."

"Drunken brothers," laughed another.

"Speak for yourself," called one of the others. "A few of us are civilized, mind you."

Simon gazed at their animated, bantering faces and the easy way they'd invited him into their fold. Brothers. As if family was not what one was born into, but instead wherever one found it. The thought was dizzying.

Several of the officers ordered food or a pint. Mr. Webb and a few others did not.

Simon turned to his secretary with a raised brow.

"Not in the mood for pigeon?"

"A gentleman is always in the mood for overcooked pigeon," Mr. Webb assured him. "My wife has one waiting at home for me, and will be sorely offended if I do not arrive with sufficient appetite as to repay her kindness in cooking for me."

Simon's smile faltered. After all the years he'd worked with Mr. Webb, he had never wondered what his home life must be like. Sure, Simon had known his secretary was a husband and a father, but he hadn't imagined him eating tough pigeon because it was all that they had.

"You should come by for dinner next week," Mr. Webb suggested, as he always did. "Perhaps Thursday?"

"Perhaps I will," Simon found himself agreeing.

His secretary's eyes lit up. "Truly?"

"May I invite a friend?" Simon asked impulsively.

"The future Mrs. Spaulding?" Mr. Webb's eyes twinkled.

"A female friend," Simon allowed grudgingly. "Headmistress at a boarding school."

Mr. Webb smiled. "Bring anyone you please. I'll even have Mrs. Webb make pudding with red currants."

Simon glanced about at the other inspectors. He wondered how many of them had a cook, or at least a small staff. Perhaps all of them. Perhaps none of them. He hadn't thought to wonder before.

He'd been so focused on the slights and disappointments being a bastard had caused, that he hadn't considered just how privileged his upbringing might have been. His father's visits to his mother were intermittent at best, but he had more than fulfilled his obligations insofar as providing his mistress with spending money and paying her bills and her retainers.

Simon had never *not* had a cook, or at least a multi-talented housekeeper. If he were forced to fend for himself in the kitchen, he was unsure he would be able to even overcook a pigeon.

That Mr. Webb had unhesitatingly invited Simon for supper on many occasions led Simon to believe that Mr. Webb's wife wasn't nearly as unskilled a cook as his joke would imply. It also meant Mr. Webb hadn't the least compunction in inviting a guest to a dinner likely to be staffed by few or any servants. Or at least, Mr. Webb didn't mind inviting Simon.

No matter how focused and task-oriented Simon became, his secretary had never ceased trying to be friends.

The other men were just as amicable, Simon quickly discovered. They regaled each other with stories of encounters on the force, poked fun at each other over laughingly recalled misadventures, and made the afternoon fly by so quickly that two hours had vanished before Simon remembered to glance at his pocket watch.

"Oh-ho!" teased one of the officers. "Spaulding is late for his day off work."

Simon grinned and shoved his watch back into his

pocket. "One of us ought to be half-competent at detecting."

"You mean because you're almost lead inspector, is that it?" said another with good-natured ribbing. "I heard the Justice of the Peace say you won't earn another promotion until you've captured the elusive Thief of Mayfair."

"Nooo," Mr. Webb moaned, dropping his head theatrically into his hands. "You've reminded him of his arch nemesis. Now he'll never take another hour off."

"The Justice of the Peace did say my next promotion hinges on finding this thief," Simon admitted. Worse, there was a ticking clock. Thanks to aristocratic pressure, the Justice of the Peace had given Simon a fortnight to solve the case—or the promotion would go to someone else. "I *will* catch him. Soon, he'll make a mistake."

"Might have last night," one of the other officers said. "Mapleton came by earlier with a list of names."

"*Phineas* Mapleton?" Simon asked.

He supposed it was no surprise. Mapleton had bragged about hosting a dinner party. Such events had thus far proved irresistible to the Thief of Mayfair.

The other inspectors grinned at each other. "Stormed in as red as a tomato, he did. Said either a jealous fop had stolen his globes, or they'd told a rival aficionado where to find them."

"Globes," Simon repeated.

He wasn't certain what was the least likely: that the Thief of Mayfair had managed to walk off with a globe in his arms in the middle of a party, or that Phineas Mapleton was an aficionado of science to begin with. Perhaps this theft was unrelated to the others.

"How many globes were stolen?" he asked.

"Four," answered one of the officers.

Simon frowned. "What did they look like? What brand? What size?"

"Mapleton hasn't the least idea," one of the other inspectors said with a grin. "Seems he kept a count, but not a list. He wouldn't recognize his own collection if it was sitting right in front of him. Can't even say for certain that it was last night. Might've been weeks ago."

"There, that should be easy to solve," said Mr. Webb with a sharp nod. "Go ahead, Inspector Spaulding. Tell us who committed the crime."

"Your tea leaves can give you as good of an answer as I can," Simon said with a shake of his head. "If it *is* the Thief of Mayfair, then it is a worrisome escalation. If it is *not* the Thief of Mayfair…"

"Then there are *two thieves of Mayfair*," breathed an officer in mock awe. "Brilliant work. I shall pen a note to the Justice of the Peace commending your sleuthing skills."

"Spaulding is never getting that promotion," sighed one of the others.

"Of course he is," Mr. Webb said staunchly. "He's the most brilliant inspector London has ever had."

"More brilliant than the Thief of Mayfair?" asked

one of the others with an arched brow.

"Let's find out." Simon pushed to his feet and tipped his hat toward the table. "I hate to leave the party, lads, but I've a criminal to catch."

He smiled to himself as he hurried back to Bow Street. His hunt for the pernicious thief had become more important than ever.

The sooner he caught the man, the sooner Simon would receive his promotion. A larger salary meant more money he could spare to help Dahlia and her school. He was no longer hunting the thief because it was his job.

He was doing it for Dahlia.

Chapter 22

"I should call off," Dahlia said in agitation as her best friend picked up the curling tongs.

"You are not calling off." Faith lifted a chunk of Dahlia's hair and expertly applied the tongs. "I am going with you. With me as your companion, it's not scandalous at all."

"It's a little scandalous," Dahlia insisted. "It's not some open-air carriage in Hyde Park. This is a private supper with Mr. Spaulding and another couple."

"It's…an unusually cozy dinner party," Faith said firmly. "Besides, you aren't invited to open-air carriages in Hyde Park anymore. Trust me, Mr. Spaulding is much better."

Dahlia winced. Her outing with her mother had made it clear that her days of attracting aristocratic bachelors were over. Or even wealthy suitors at all.

Her new, lower status was still close enough to the

fringes for begging donations from old friends, but there would be no prince sweeping in to save her and her school from financial ruin.

She would have to do that herself.

"Are you certain you wish to play chaperone?" Dahlia bit her lip. "As much as I appreciate the help, I would hate for you to suffer through what might be an incredibly awkward evening."

"What else do I have on my calendar?" Faith replied lightly. "There's no need to worry about my reputation. Your set doesn't send me invitations anyway."

Dahlia grimaced. After tonight, she would redouble her efforts to mind her place in society so that she too didn't stop receiving invitations. Future donations depended on her maintaining those ties.

"My mother wanted me to marry for money," she said after a moment. "Particularly if it involved a title. She's quite disappointed it won't happen."

"Don't all mothers want that?" Faith moved to the next section of hair. "What do *you* want?"

Dahlia closed her eyes. The fact that she had spent the past hour primping for a dinner with Simon answered that question on its own, and her best friend knew it.

"I want to keep the school open for as long as humanly possible," she said instead. Both answers were true. One was simply more important than the other. "I want to bequeath the school to a new headmistress when I die. I want opportunities like this to always exist for girls who need them."

"Are you saying you're uninterested in Mr. Spaulding?"

"I'm saying I can't have him. Not when I need to nurture what few connections I have left," Dahlia replied with a sigh. "I almost wish I *had* married for money. Everyone thinks it's more important than love, and in this case maybe it is. I cannot help but have more sympathy for—"

Faith stopped fixing hair.

"No sympathy," Dahlia said quickly. "No sympathy at all. He's a cretin. A selfish, boorish cad. He should never have cared about your position in society or your lack of dowry. A pox on his soul! I hope his valet ties his cravat so tight that he faints face-first into a bowl of cold porridge in front of the entire ton."

The hurt expression didn't leave Faith's face, but she began curling her hair again.

Dahlia's shoulders sagged. She hadn't meant to allude to the sins in Hawkridge's past, or the daily burden it had caused for Faith. Yet the parallels were uncomfortably clear.

The only recourse was to behave completely unlike the marquess. She would be friendly to Simon, but not romantical. The kisses had been a mistake. Delicious, toe-curling, intoxicating mistakes.

But she liked Simon too much to promise him a future they could not have. As much as she enjoyed their clandestine kisses, if the choices were formal courtship or simple friendship…then they would have to remain friends. She would have to avoid private interludes after this.

No matter how difficult that would be.

"The girls enjoyed mathematics class today," Faith said in an obvious attempt to change the subject.

"They love role-playing." Dahlia grinned. "I had them take turns playing flower girl and serving wench to practice making change and doing sums in one's head."

"*You* love role-playing," Faith corrected, her voice fond. "I watched you interrupt every transaction by pretending to be an irate customer. I can't say I've ever seen someone cartwheel about a fruit stand before."

Dahlia cleared her throat with an unrepentant smile. That had been her favorite part. "Life is an endless string of distractions. They must be able to add and subtract correctly no matter what might be going on about them. Besides, I could use the practice. If this headmistress bit doesn't work out, I may need to join the circus."

"Every one of those girls would join right along with you." Faith set down the tongs and began arranging ringlets with pearl combs. "You ought to teach circus class to those who want more exercise."

"Circus class," Dahlia breathed with growing excitement. "Faith, you're a genius! The girls could put on a small acrobatics performance to raise funds and build awareness about the school. Who doesn't love the circus? And impish little girls? Society ladies will practically throw pound notes at the stage."

"At a troupe of street children in trousers?" Faith asked doubtfully.

"We can sort out the details," Dahlia assured her. Already the idea was taking root.

If the donations raised were anywhere near what she hoped, perhaps the girls could put on a small show every season—or every month! Heaven knew aristocrats considered themselves aficionados of all performing arts, from the grand opera to family musicales. Why not acrobatics?

With luck, the school could start to earn enough funds to keep Dahlia from ever being forced to play Robin Hood again. Excitement rushed through her blood. How much time would be required to choreograph a reasonably competent performance? Three months? Two? She only had to stretch pennies until then. Hope buoyed her spirits.

She could do this. *They* could do this.

"Once we start raising more than we spend, we can remodel the rest of the abbey." She couldn't stop smiling. "Not all at once. One room at a time."

"Possibly even take in a few paying students to offset the cost," Faith suggested.

Dahlia nodded. She wasn't convinced that parents who could afford boarding school tuition would want their offspring rubbing shoulders with destitute children…but perhaps that was because she was still thinking like the daughter of a baroness.

As a mere trade mogul, Faith's father had sent her to the finest institution that would accept her. Undoubtedly there would be families who couldn't afford what the ton might consider a proper boarding school—or even the wages of an independent tutor. They might leap at the chance to give their children an education they could not otherwise afford.

"Thirty days has come and gone," she said as Faith stepped back to admire her handiwork. "You've seen the school. You've met the girls. Please say you'll stay on permanently. I can have a barrister transfer fifty percent ownership this very week."

Faith bit her lip. "I have so many obligations at home—"

"I know you do," Dahlia said quickly. "I would never come between them. Your schedule can be as flexible as you need."

"Let me finish," Faith chided with a fond shake of her head. "You always rush into everything you do without taking a moment to breathe. I was going to say that I see my situation at home as complementary to the potential here. You know how much I love children. I cannot imagine walking away from these girls or this cause. I shall be honored to consider this school my own."

Dahlia leapt up from her chair to envelop Faith in a fierce embrace.

Not only would she start the official transfer first

thing in the morning, she would have her brother Heath hold on to a second document bequeathing the entirety of her portion to Faith in the event Dahlia was run over by a carriage—or forced by circumstances to wed. Unlike their unmarried counterparts, wives could not own property. Dahlia couldn't risk having a husband decide not to allow her to support the school. It would be unfair to Faith, and disastrous for the children.

"You are the very best," she informed Faith with feeling.

Faith swung her hands in a dramatic *Who, me?* gesture, then grinned. "I know. Now, that's enough saving the world for one day. Someone is waiting for you to join him. A certain handsome inspector whose gruff, straight-and-narrow exterior cannot begin to hide the heat in his smoldering eyes every time he looks in your direction."

"Really, Faith. Smoldering eyes?" Dahlia said weakly, as her heart thumped in total agreement. Just thinking about Simon sent a frisson from her spine to her core. "Let's go hire a hackney."

When they arrived at the address, the front door flung open to reveal a short, jovial looking man with ruddy cheeks and kind eyes.

"You must be Inspector Spaulding's friends," he said merrily. "Do come in. I am Mr. Webb. Inspector Spaulding is already at the table, and Mrs. Webb will be joining us shortly."

Inspector Spaulding was not at the table. Simon had materialized behind Mr. Webb's shoulder within moments of their host opening the door.

"Good evening, Miss Grenville, Miss Digby." Simon's low voice had addressed both ladies, but his fathomless blue eyes focused wholly on Dahlia.

Any reply she might have made was trapped somewhere behind her rapidly beating heart. It was unpardonably rude to ignore her host in order to drink in the sight of a tall, dark, deliciously buttoned-up inspector, but her eyes could look nowhere else. It had been days since last she'd seen him. Days since his warm, firm lips had claimed her own.

Now here he was.

If the mere thought of seeing him sent butterflies to her stomach, finally having him within reach—and still being unable to touch him—had every nerve ending electric with awareness. She would not be able to eat. Not when the only thing she hungered for were the return of Simon's kisses.

Faith looped her arm through Dahlia's and all but dragged her to the dinner table.

"Stop it," she whispered as she forced Dahlia's weak knees into the closest chair. "I've lost every scrap of my innocence just from *watching* the two of you devour each other with your eyes."

"You're not innocent," Dahlia muttered as her trembling hands fumbled for a serviette.

"Which means I know precisely what you're thinking," Faith reminded her as she smoothed out her own serviette. "Devouring happens in private. You will owe me an obscenely large favor, but I promise to aid you in procuring a few moments' privacy the next time your inspector pays a call... provided that the two of you refrain from melting his colleague's supper chairs from all of your heated glances."

Colleague.

Dahlia snapped up straight. Stealing an hour or two of Simon's company was not the only reason she was here tonight. She was also meant to make a positive impression on Simon's friends.

Although she and Simon were not destined for a future together, he was on course for a long and decorated career. The last thing she desired was to make his work environment awkward in any way.

Or to let on how nervous being in a room with not one but *two* Bow Street employees made her.

She smiled at Mr. Webb. "Thank you for opening your home to us. Your dinner invitation is most kind."

"And overdue," came a merry voice as a rosy-cheeked woman bearing a platter of roasted meat emerged from the kitchen. "I have been after Mr. Webb for years to invite Inspector Spaulding to supper. We are delighted that he has brought guests."

Dahlia's gaze snapped down the table to Simon's. He'd requested her presence at the first invitation he'd ever received?

He shook his head. "I am afraid the fault is mine. Your husband has been tempting me with tales of your fine cooking since the day we met. It is rare that I find myself with neither a dossier nor a prisoner in hand."

"Wholly understandable," Mr. Webb said firmly. "One becomes on the verge of being the highest-ranking inspector in Bow Street history through dedicated and impeccable police-work, not from accepting idle social engagements."

"I, for one, am rather fond of idle social engagements," Mrs. Webb said with a wink in Faith and Dahlia's direction. "If you lads would rather return to your dark, dusty offices, I am certain we ladies can find *some* use for the new bottle of port in your study."

"Never. Again," Mr. Webb bit out with such horror that Dahlia couldn't help but grin.

Mrs. Webb already sounded like the sort of smart, mischievous woman Dahlia absolutely loved to befriend.

The first course blurred into the second amid a constant stream of laughter and jovial conversation. Dahlia's cheeks ached so much from nonstop smiling and verbal parries that she marveled any of them had been able to consume any of the meal at all.

"We *must* do this again." Mrs. Webb placed a bowl of pudding with red currants in the center of the table. "Please don't say I must wait another ten years before my husband can sweet talk you three into returning."

"Surely it hasn't been ten years," Simon protested.

"Eleven," Mr. Webb murmured innocently. "But who's counting?"

Dahlia grinned. If there weren't accounts to pay, mouths to feed, and a school to run, Dahlia would have happily agreed to dine with this witty, irreverent crowd every day, if they so desired. She could not recall the last time she'd had such fun at a supper engagement.

Her spoon paused halfway to her serving of pudding. It was true. She could *not* recall the last time she'd had so much fun at a dinner party, outside of her own family.

Dahlia's list of past supper invitations read like a guide to *Debrett's Peerage*, and yet the most enjoyable evening she'd spent around a dining table was not the sampling of delicate sauces created by a chef poached from French aristocrats or the stilted conversation of competing debutantes with little more in common than having been seated together by rank.

It was here. It was now. The best social engagement of her life was a handful of sharp-witted, title-less, ordinary people sharing a night of friendship and laughter around a bowl of currant pudding.

Her mother would be horrified.

Dahlia was glad she had kept her rank a secret. Society believed daughters of baronesses to have been born unsurpassably superior to the invisible ants of the working class.

What if the Webbs believed her an uppity toff who

considered herself too good for the likes of them? What if Simon chose to honor their class differences by never speaking to her again, outside of his professional capacity?

She knew how he felt about his brother. How Simon's father had treated him and his mother. The last thing she wanted was for him to lump her in that same group.

Yet she had been raised to understand that was precisely what ought to happen. Countesses and harried footmen might both be inside Almack's at the same time, but they weren't there to be friends. One was meant to serve. The other was meant to enjoy.

The rules were no more the patronesses of Almack's fault than they were her mother's. From slaves to kings, the world had been divided into class-based strata since time immemorial. Society honoring those distinctions was far from shocking. Dahlia hiding her identity, on the other hand, would scandalize far more than the fashionable set if the truth were to come to light. She might not see Simon again.

It was not a complete lie, she assured herself. After all, she was not currently a *practicing* baroness's daughter. She was...a simple headmistress.

And part-time thief. She swallowed uncomfortably.

"What do you say?" Simon's smile bathed her in warmth. "Might your schedule allow for another such gathering at some point in the future?"

She wanted to say yes. Of course she wished to say

yes. Instead, she stared back at him wordlessly.

Up until now, Dahlia had been so concerned about improving her girls' lives, that she hadn't had time to have a life of her own. She could not dare risk her thin ties to society by allowing a courtship—or even public knowledge of association with friends like these—but it was nice to have a private moment to do with as she pleased.

She could not make a habit of dinner parties at the home of a Bow Street secretary, but it was harder and harder to resist the allure of clandestine kisses in the arms of a certain inspector.

The more she fought her attraction to Simon, the more she dreaded the inevitability of giving him up.

He deserved to find a nice young lady who would wed him and dedicate her life to *him*, not a charity. And Dahlia couldn't risk allowing him—or the law—to come between her and her school. Twenty-four wards were counting on her.

"I don't know why you're asking poor Miss Grenville if there's room in her agenda, when it's you who never has a moment to spare on frivolity," Mr. Webb said, eyes twinkling. "How will you ever get your promotion if you halt your breakneck schedule for something so mundane as *eating?*"

"Promotion?" Faith raised a saucy brow. "I assumed he was the highest-ranking inspector on Bow Street. I feel so betrayed."

"Almost," Simon demurred. "Once I close one of my more insidious open cases, I am promised a new title. It's nothing, really."

Dahlia's lips curved. Perhaps the classes weren't so different after all. Nothing was worth more than a title.

"And a spot of reward money," Mr. Webb said as if it were only just occurring to him. "And a pay increase. Oh, and a public commendation. Nothing, really. It's not as if your career depends on it."

"I would catch this criminal even if it did not." Simon's eyes were cold enough to chill the air. "He shall never leave Newgate."

Dahlia shivered. "Is London home to a murderer?"

"Often, unfortunately," said Mr. Webb. "But don't you fear. Inspector Spaulding catches all criminals, no matter the crime. The current focus is merely a thief."

"Not 'merely,'" Simon growled. "The carelessness of thieves can cause just as grievous harm as a murderer. Most of the violence I see every night is due to altercations with footpads."

"I do apologize," Mr. Webb said with a glance at his wife. "I should not have mentioned work matters in front of ladies."

"Nonsense," Mrs. Webb said briskly. "I'm certain all the ladies at this table are aware of the dangers of footpads. You've only to open a newspaper to see the latest tale of highwaymen and other unsavories. We are lucky to have men like you rid the city of the bad element."

Dahlia smiled at Simon, despite the uneasy flutter in

her belly. "You risk your life for others every single night. The least they can give you is an improved title and a bit of a reward. You're a hero. I've known it since the day we met."

He shrugged away the compliment. "It's my job. Once the Thief of Mayfair is off to the gallows, I can return to protecting all citizens of London, rather than chasing down pocket globes and miniature harps."

Pocket globes. Miniature harps. Dahlia froze in horror as she realized the awful truth. God save her.

Simon wasn't hunting "a" thief.

He was hunting *her*.

Chapter 23

The last thing Simon had wanted was to walk into the Cloven Hoof and all but trip over his brother.

The good news—if, indeed, there was anything good at all about the current situation—was that with Hawkridge's well-tailored back toward Simon, the marquess hadn't noticed his illegitimate half-brother at all.

Hardly an ironic turn of events, Simon acknowledged from a dark corner of the main room.

Hawkridge had made an art form out of self-absorption. For years, Simon's younger self had dreamed of surprising his sure-to-be delighted brother with his existence, only to discover the younger marquess had always known and never cared.

As for the previous marquess going so far as to boast about his bastard in order to manipulate his legitimate son... Well. Simon rather thought the bastard was their father. Although perhaps the old marquess wasn't all bad. Simon had always assumed his father had deposited money for him and his mother out of the same sense of duty one might pay one's cobbler or one's tailor.

The idea that perhaps it wasn't as black-and-white as that was mind-blowing. His father might actually have possessed a modicum of affection for both of his sons.

Simon had never touched the old account that had been left in his name because he would rather have his self-respect than a fleet of phaetons. If there was even enough for flashy purchases. He hadn't looked at the balance in over a decade.

He made a mental note to have his solicitor make a few inquiries. Perhaps there would be enough to outfit Dahlia's girls with new dresses and shoes that fit.

Once his promotion came through, he'd be able to do even more.

He settled into a shadowy nook in the Cloven Hoof and pushed his personal concerns from his mind. He was here to investigate Maxwell Gideon. Simon would view his half-brother's presence not as a sharp reminder of unresolved family matters, but as emblematic of the sort of clientele Gideon sought to attract.

As luck would have it, Hawkridge's decision to visit a gentlemen's club of suspicious financial background on this particular evening was actually a boon to Simon's investigation. The last few times he'd visited, the owner of the gambling den had either been off-premises, or hidden away in a back room, doing God-knew-what.

Not tonight.

Maxwell Gideon had been *en route* from the gaming tables to the passageway leading to his office when Hawkridge entered the club. Gideon spun an immediate about-face to join both Hawkridge and their friend Lord Wainwright at what was clearly the trio's customary table.

Despite a visceral disinterest in knowing any details about his half-brother's life, Simon would be forced to listen carefully, lest any hint of the club owner's suspicious dealings enter the conversation. With a sigh, he tilted an ear toward the table.

"Lovely caricature of you in the morning paper," Hawkridge commented to Lord Wainwright. "Something about, 'his countess's voice turns the Lord of Pleasure into a Puddle of Pleasure even after months of marriage,' if I recall correctly?"

The earl's hallmark rakish smile only widened. "And yet there was no mention of you in any of the pages. The hunt for an heiress must be going slower than planned. Oh my, I didn't realize a marquess could find himself on the shelf."

"Outright trickery does seem to be the only way for you to get a woman of quality to the altar," Gideon put in helpfully.

"Thank you." Hawkridge rolled his eyes. "Always a gentleman. I shall take your suggestion to heart, should more ethical methods prove fruitless."

Wainwright brightened. "With luck, your bamboozled heiress will be a halfwit and hideously ugly."

Hawkridge slanted the earl a flat look. "How is my marrying some repulsive idiot 'lucky?'"

"Oh, not for *you*." Wainwright straightened his shirt points beneath razor sharp cheekbones with exaggerated precision. "For *me*. One gets so tired of the society papers going on and on about how dreadfully happy, attractive, and in love one is with one's wife. You being stuck with some rich, featherbrained shrew would be a refreshing change of pace, wouldn't you say?"

"Absolutely," Gideon agreed before Hawkridge could reply. "We're *all* tired of hearing how blissful, attractive, and in love the two of you are. Since Hawkridge is sacrificing his future happiness anyway, he might as well do so in whichever way most amuses his fellow man. It's positively patriotic."

Hawkridge's smile flashed before clenched teeth. "Do you know what would amuse *me?*"

The arrival of a barmaid fortunately saved both Wainwright and Gideon from whatever blistering setdown Hawkridge had planned.

Despite the bitterness Simon had long held toward his brother, he could not repress a flash of pity. Inheriting a destitute marquessate left Hawkridge no choice but to wed any given woman in possession of the largest dowry.

Whereas Simon was born with a variety of choices

Hawkridge would never have. Simon had the freedom to fall in love, to find employment he enjoyed, to marry the woman he loved—or, if he so chose, to never wed at all. The most important decisions any man would ever face were completely up to Simon, in a way that those same decisions would never be up to Hawkridge. A marquess's job was being a marquess. Marrying a certain class of woman who possessed a certain level of money.

No matter what the marquess's heart might desire.

Simon, on the other hand, could do as he pleased. No, an officer of the law could not woo some high society debutante. But within his own class, Simon could wed whomever he wanted. The only prerequisite was that the woman also want him.

He forced the memory of soft, pink lips and large, expressive eyes from his mind. He was here to observe a club owner, not moon over a trouser-wearing headmistress.

"Don't be ridiculous," Gideon was saying to Hawkridge. "Let me buy you a glass of wine."

"I told you," Hawkridge bit out, his cheeks flushing. "No charity. I'll buy my own wine or I won't have any at all."

"Wainwright!" shouted voices from over near the Hazard table. "Gideon! Come put a crown on Underhill's next roll. He's had three eleven's in a row!"

Laughing, both men rose from the table and disappeared into the milieu to see what the ruckus was about.

Hawkridge remained behind, a single man at an

empty table.

Simon presumed the reason the marquess hadn't moved was the same reason his name hadn't been called with the others. He didn't have a crown. He didn't have tuppence. Every visit to see his friends was likely one more deathblow against his pride.

Blast. Simon rubbed his temples. He couldn't leave his brother sitting there, alone in a crowded club. Stoic despite the slights.

He was going to have to extend an olive branch.

In all likelihood, Hawkridge would bat away any attempt at patching up the insurmountable differences between them. But Simon had never backed down from doing what was right.

Dahlia had pointed out whether Simon and his brother lived out the rest of their lives as strangers was largely up to Simon. Hawkridge had been in a stormy mood even before Simon had blocked his path to force an introduction. The marquess did not shoulder complete fault for how disastrously that conversation had turned out.

Simon had avoided this moment long enough. A man of strong character would not hesitate to apologize for his portion of the blame. He pushed to his feet with a sigh.

At least Hawkridge had no drink to toss in his face.

Simon approached the marquess's table well aware

of the infinite other possibilities for embarrassment. Unlike last time, they were not in the private enclave between the gaming section and the back office. Hawkridge was seated at a rear table in the primary salon. Halfway between the bar and the Faro tables. In direct sight of anyone entering the club.

In direct sight of *everyone* currently in the club, as a matter of fact.

Hawkridge glanced up as Simon neared the table. The marquess's eyes widened in recognition.

Simon cleared his throat to make room for a difficult apology. "I—"

"Sit," Hawkridge interrupted. "Don't loom over me like a mathematics tutor when there are perfectly fine seats all around this table."

Simon blinked. "Your friends—"

"Are betting on the toss of the dice," Hawkridge finished. "If he wagers a crown a minute, Wainwright will be dead before he runs out of fortune. *Sit*. If he misses his chair, he can buy another."

Simon sat.

"I suppose I should be glad you're here," Hawkridge continued moodily. "I owed you an apology and really disliked the idea of having to present myself at Bow Street just to deliver it."

If any other peer had made that statement, Simon would have assumed apologizing in a place as public as the court would have been too embarrassing. Yet here they were, in a far more crowded room, among far more important and well-connected individuals.

Simon tilted his head. "Why?"

"Oh, you know why." Hawkridge sighed. "I was beastly to you the other day and you didn't deserve it. In my defense, you could not have possibly had worse timing. But in *your* defense… I doubt much would have changed. After all, I've been jealous of you since the day I learned of your existence."

A marquess jealous of Simon. The idea still boggled. "When did you learn of me?"

Hawkridge leaned forward, his smile humorless. "I don't even know. I can't remember not knowing. Perhaps I heard my parents arguing, or perhaps it was never a secret at all. How about you? When did you find out?"

"I never didn't know," Simon admitted. "I suppose it was the same. You were a fact, just like two shillings in a florin or two ten bobs in a pound."

Hawkridge lifted his brows. "You *are* like a maths tutor. I thought I was jesting."

"Is it more fun if I'm a Latin tutor?" Simon asked innocently. "I can have you decline a few verbs."

Hawkridge shuddered. "At least figures are useful. I haven't conjugated Latin since Oxford, and I aspire to keep it that way, if you don't mind."

Simon grinned despite himself…and suddenly realized he was bantering with a marquess in the middle of an exclusive gentlemen's club as if they were equals.

Something they could never be.

"You deserve an apology from me as well," he said, before he lost sight of the reason he'd approached the table.

"Do I?" Hawkridge's smile was crooked. "I thought so, when I was younger. When it felt like you got everything."

"What 'everything?'" Simon burst out in disbelief. "You got his name. His *title*."

"But you got him," Hawkridge said simply. "We weren't his real family. You were."

"It doesn't get realer than inheriting a marquessate."

"Doesn't it? We had him for stolen moments here and there, when he wasn't busy with the House of Lords…or whisking you and your mother off to the countryside."

"Holidays like that were rare." And, ultimately, fatal. Simon pushed away the memory. "He took you riding every day."

"I took daily rides with a horse he purchased me," Hawkridge corrected. "It's not quite the same as having company on the ride."

"I was so jealous of you." Simon raked his fingers through his hair as he stared at the marquess. "*So* jealous."

"You'll probably think I'm lying if I say I used to dream of switching places with you." Hawkridge scoffed self-deprecatingly. "Poor little rich lad, and all that."

"Except you aren't rich," Simon said softly.

Hawkridge inclined his head. "I am not."

Simon leaned back. What if the line that had always separated them was as much their own fault as society's?

"Our births were so close, we were practically born twins." He hesitated. "Why do I feel like we've wasted every moment of the two-and-thirty years since that day?"

"Not every moment." Hawkridge lifted a palm. "We're here now, aren't we?"

"At a questionably legal gaming establishment," Simon said, deadpan.

"Where neither of us is gambling," Hawkridge agreed, neither denying nor confirming the questionable legal status of the venue. "Next to a bar possessing some of the finest wines in London."

"Which neither of us is drinking," Simon finished. He motioned to the barmaid. "I can fix that, at least."

Hawkridge snapped up straight in obvious offense. "I hope you're buying yourself a drink."

"I don't drink on duty. That would be irresponsible." Simon glanced up at the approaching barmaid. "Please bring this prickly sot your finest glass of whatever he's having."

"Nothing," Hawkridge bit out. "I'm having nothing. I won't accept charity from my friends and I won't accept it from you."

"That's right. I'm not your friend. And this isn't charity." Simon slammed his palm to the table. "I'll buy you all the bloody drinks I want. You're my little brother.

What else is family for?"

Hawkridge stared back at him for a long moment without blinking.

"By accepting a drink, I'm either accepting charity...or a brother." The marquess lifted his nose. "I refuse to accept charity."

Simon shrugged a shoulder. "Stay thirsty, then. Have it your way."

"I will." Hawkridge smiled up at the barmaid. "Two cups of tea if you would, Jemima. My brother doesn't drink when he's on duty." The marquess lowered his voice to an exaggerated whisper. "He thinks it's irresponsible."

Jemima winked and set off in search of a teapot.

"Next time, it's wine," Hawkridge warned Simon. "Sipping tea in the middle of a gentlemen's club is bound to hurt my image."

"It's not hurting your image," Simon protested. "I'm helping you. Now the heiresses will think you can afford tea."

Hawkridge stroked his chin. "That's a fair point. Ladies do like tea. Perhaps Jemima is a secret heiress."

"She also knows you can't afford tea," Simon reminded him. "To her, *I* look like the better deal."

Jemima returned with a steaming tea service. "Anything else, gentlemen?"

"Just one thing." Hawkridge raised his china teacup and grinned at Simon. "To the next thirty years?"

"To the next thirty," Simon agreed as he clinked the

painted rim of his cup with his brother's.

Chapter 24

Despite the riotous sounds, smells, and colors of the Covent Garden Market, Simon strolled through the chaotic maze of donkeys, fruit stands, and costermongers as if he'd never experienced a more peaceful afternoon walk. Life felt like it was finally on the perfect track.

After sharing a pot of tea at the Cloven Hoof, he and his brother had not exchanged locks of hair or anything so romantic, but an important corner had clearly been turned.

He and his brother were *speaking*.

They might never be the sort of friends who went riding together or retired for a week or two at a hunting box in the country, but Simon didn't care about any of that. He didn't have *time* for any of that. Sharing a table now and again for an hour's chat free of rancor or animosity, on the other hand... Well, that was a gift he'd long ago stopped believing in.

And he owed it all to Dahlia.

A smile teased Simon's lips as her image filled his mind. Since the day he'd been orphaned, Simon had believed himself alone in the world. Dahlia had proved him wrong time and again.

First, there was her. He wasn't quite certain at what point he'd stopped being able to imagine a future without her in it, but, well, there it was. She was a part of him now.

As were the students at her boarding school. The weekly dancing lessons had taught him as much as it had taught the girls. By dancing with each one of them, week after week, he'd not only learned their names, their histories, their fears, their dreams... He'd become part of their family.

Nor was the St. Giles School for Girls his only family. His colleagues at Bow Street were another, even if he'd been too blind to see it until now. Having an after-work drink with the others wasn't about imbibing gin, but about sharing a sense of brotherhood. The officers weren't in competition. They were a team. Fighting to achieve the same goal: a safer London. If they ended up making friends in the process, what was the harm in that?

Simon now looked forward to work as much for the updates in their various lives as in their cases. Rarely did a day pass by without one of the inspectors regaling the others with tales of a misadventure, or the wise and pithy comments of a wife who was more than obviously his equal.

That he could blend both worlds had seemed a miracle in its own right. Having Dahlia and the Webbs seated around the same table had heralded one of the most delightful evenings of his life. The thought of continuing to enjoy their company for the *rest* of his life would make any man feel like the most fortunate soul on earth.

To have a *brother* on top of it all… It was positively dizzying, this good fortune. Each day better than the one before! Simon could scarcely wait to see Dahlia and tell her all about it.

Initially, he'd had a conversation of another sort in mind. Had bought a ring. Been carrying it around for days, waiting for the right time. Waiting for the right *words*.

He had always known that if he ever found the right woman, he would marry her. It wasn't so much the legalities of the matter, as the emotional toll. Because Simon's father had never recognized him as his son, not even as an accidental by-blow, Simon had always believed the old marquess to be ashamed of him. Not just him—of he and his mother both.

By stringing his mother along all those years, the marquess had not only withheld any sense of belonging from his illegitimate son, he had also prevented Simon's mother from moving on. His constant, inconstant presence had blocked Simon and his mother both from ever having the opportunity to find a real family. A step-father who would have acknowledged Simon's existence, loved Simon's mother, and possibly even been proud of them both.

But all of that was about *Simon*. He had never considered himself to be a particularly romantic man, but he was wise enough to realize that "I'm marrying you to legitimize any accidental offspring" lacked a certain *je ne sais quoi* when it came to compelling proposals.

Dahlia wasn't going to marry him because of his childhood. She was going to marry him because… Because…

His hands went clammy. *This* was why he had not yet asked the question. He knew why he wanted to marry *her*—he loved her mind, her heart, her fearlessness, her kisses—but why in heaven's name would she want to marry *him*?

He worked far too much with no intention of stopping, he had a past that still haunted him, complicated feelings about the people in his present, the only thing he knew about his future was that he couldn't imagine a moment of it without the woman he loved right beside… Right…

Simon's throat convulsed. The woman he loved. He was in *love* with her. That was all he had to say, the entire bloody proposal wrapped up in three little words, and yet he could think of nothing more terrifying to say. It would be like slicing open his heart and presenting her with the ceremonial dagger, then waiting to see whether she would heal him or keep slicing.

She would say yes, wouldn't she? Of course she would say yes. What woman didn't wish to be loved?

Then again, there was always the possibility that she didn't love *him*. That while she did indeed long to receive just such a passionate proposal from a smitten suitor, she'd rather hoped some other chap would be the one doing the asking. Perhaps a nice vicar, with plenty of time to help at the school and a passel of philanthropic parishioners.

Or a tutor. Wouldn't a tutor be better than an inspector? Some angel-faced genius who conjugated verbs in his sleep and painted stunning portraits with his eyes closed. The sort of fellow who could give every one of Dahlia's indigent schoolgirls an education to rival the daughters of dukes and earls.

Flowers. Simon should start with flowers. He *would* ask Dahlia for her hand in marriage—he'd bought the ring, hadn't he?—but there was no reason to rush headlong into something as serious as a proposal. He needed her to say yes. He needed *her*, blast it all.

As soon as he could determine exactly how to bare his heart to best advantage, he would do so straight away. Simon wasn't a dillydallying sort of man. He certainly wasn't afraid of a simple question. He was simply cautious, that's all. And until the right moment came along...

"Primroses, two bundles for a penny!" came the

plaintive cry of one of the many flower girls snaking through Covent Garden. She couldn't be than his elbow, yet hefted a basket almost as big as she was.

Simon planted himself in her path. "I'll take them."

She smiled in delight. "How many flowers would you like, sir?"

"A dozen," he said decisively. "No—two dozen. They're fresh, aren't they?"

"Cut them this very morn," the flower girl assured him as she counted off the stems.

Simon doubted that very much, but what did it matter? He was in the market for flowers, and these were stunningly beautiful. White, heart-shaped petals. Warm, golden-yellow centers. A sweet, subtle scent.

A far less subtle message.

A single primrose was romantic. A dozen was very romantic. Two dozen pristine primroses said *I probably have a ring in my pocket.* Depending on Dahlia's response to the flowers, perhaps today would be the day she made him the happiest man alive.

He bought a scrap of cloth to keep the primroses safe from the wind, then raced from the market to St. Giles as fast as his horse could carry him.

With his heart beating so hard it was likely shaking his cravat, Simon slid off his horse, made his way to the boarding school door, and banged the knocker.

No one came.

After an interminable wait, Simon banged the

knocker a second time. Harder. The dreaded "inspector knock."

Still nothing.

Perhaps they weren't at home. Perhaps he had worked his horse and himself into a lather only to have to return to his empty house with two dozen primroses that would wilt by morning because he hadn't the least idea how to take care of them.

He reached out and tried the door handle. It was unlocked.

With the gentlest of pushes, the door swung open with nary a creak. Simon quickly stepped inside and shut the door behind him. Now what?

Soft thuds and excited voices emanated from the rear chamber where the students gathered for their weekly dance lessons. Tonight wasn't dance night, but clearly some other exercise-based activity was currently underway. He crept forward, pausing just outside the open doorway.

The good news was that Dahlia led the school's exercise program, which meant the object of his affection was right on the other side of the wall.

The bad news was that so was a crowded ballroom full of pinafored witnesses.

He took a deep breath, lifted the flowers, and strode through the doorway. Every pair of eyes swung to face him in shock.

To be fair, Simon was doing the same thing.

Not only was the woman he hoped would become

his future bride turning somersaults across the frayed center carpet in a pair of men's trousers…

So were all of her students.

Trousers. Somersaults. Definitely not dance lessons. Simon forced a smile. "Er… Good evening, ladies."

Dahlia was the first to bounce to her feet. "Mr. Spaulding! Always a lovely surprise. What brings you here tonight?"

Given the ostentatious waterfall of spring primroses blossoming from his fist, Simon reckoned he'd lost any element of surprise. Nothing left to do but continue the mission as planned.

He cleared his throat. Onward, then. "You must know that my heart has been stolen…"

The elder half of the trousered schoolgirls clapped a hand to their mouth or their chest in disbelief and anticipation. The younger half of the female tumblers simply stared at him in wide-eyed bafflement.

Simon swallowed. Some of these children believed they were about to witness the most romantic spectacle of their lives. The others hadn't witnessed enough gallantry to even recognize it unfold before them. Before being welcomed into Dahlia's school, most of the children had never previously been shown kindness. He straightened.

Flowers weren't the way to Dahlia's heart. Nor was this moment about the two of them.

He swept into the room with renewed purpose.

"Miss Grenville, would you please hold out your hand?"

She did so with a bemused smile.

"Thank you." He handed her his hat. "As I was saying, my heart has been stolen by a cadre of shameless young ladies. I am here to give a flower to every woman in possession of a bit of my heart, to let her know that I see what she has done…and that she may keep it. I find myself love-struck by the entire trouser-wearing lot of them."

He turned to Molly, who stared up at him with shocked blue eyes.

"You, above all, must have the first primrose. If it were not for you, I would never have been introduced to the St. Giles School for Girls in the first place. I owe you far more than my heart." He handed her a flower.

She clutched it to her chest without a word.

He turned to the next girl. "Louisa, it was the greatest honor of my life to loan you my greatcoat when you required its warmth. Even though you have rudely failed to see to its safe return, I remain quite smitten by your smile. This primrose is for you."

She accepted it with jittery fingers.

Child by child, Simon made his way about the large chamber. Each flower was given along with a compliment by name and a personal comment, ensuring each girl realized her flower was for *her*. They were not invisible. They were important. They mattered to him. They mattered in their own right.

Only when he was down to the last few primroses

did Simon realize he had made a slight miscalculation at the time of his purchase. He had enough flowers for every girl in the ballroom... but there wouldn't be any left for Dahlia.

After the final primrose had been given away, he slowly turned to face her.

Her beautiful dark eyes glistened with unshed tears.

"Just because I don't have any flowers left," he stammered, "doesn't mean the biggest part of my heart belongs to anyone but y—"

She tossed his hat to the carpet and threw herself into his arms.

"You daft man." she said as she pressed a damp cheek to his neck. "Everyone's hearts belong to you."

"Kiss him!" shouted one of the girls, to much whooping from the others.

Simon slid a hand into his waistcoat pocket. He touched the ring and took a deep breath. This was the moment. He need only sink to one knee.

"Dahlia," he said, his voice shaking as much as his fingers. "There's just one more thing."

Chapter 25

A movement in the doorway caught Dahlia's eye. *Faith!* Thank God.

"Miss Digby," she called out before Faith could trudge up the stairs. "What perfect timing. You do recall that favor you owe me?"

Privacy? Faith mouthed silently, eyebrows raised in portent.

Immediately, Dahlia mouthed back, tilting her head toward two dozen delighted schoolgirls. "Ladies, Miss Digby will now cover the operational aspects of Circus Minimus while I have a brief chat with Mr. Spaulding."

"I just want to say…" Simon paused and his knee seemed to buckle.

Dahlia grabbed him by the elbow and hauled him out of the ballroom. "Not here."

In fact, she didn't want to waste time with talking at all. From the moment she had realized he was going to be empty-handed after his incredibly sweet gesture, all she could think about was filling his arms with her body.

"Where are we going?" he asked as she all but dragged him up the staircase. "To your office?"

"Yes," wasn't a complete lie. It wasn't her fault the abbey's small size meant her office and her bedchamber were now the same room.

He was too good for her. She recognized that. She intended to change it. For starters, as soon as the Circus Minimus amassed sufficient donations, she would never go back to being a thief again. She now had a business partner. A plan for raising money.

And for the first time: hope.

The rest of her situation hadn't changed. The school still balanced on the edge of financial ruin. Until the donations far outweighed expenses, she could not dare jeopardize her position in society with the barest hint of scandal—such as a romantic involvement with a Bow Street Runner.

But just because there could be no courtship didn't mean they couldn't be together for just one night. There was no one she would rather have clandestine affair with than Simon. Heat-of-the-moment kisses and secret embraces were far from enough.

She flung open her door, pulled him inside, and turned the key in the lock.

His brow furrowed only briefly before he seemed to

take heart. "Dahlia, it would bring me the greatest pleasure if—"

She rose up on her toes and pressed her lips to his.

Her heart pounded. She knew exactly what would bring them the greatest pleasure. She hooked her hands about his lapels and tumbled backward onto her mattress, bringing him with her.

"I…" he began again. "That is, would you…"

She sank her fingers into his hair and kissed him with all the abandonment of her heart.

He either forgot whatever he'd been about to say, or finally realized there were far better uses for their mouths than wasting them on conversation.

Kissing him within the privacy of her locked bedchamber was even more thrilling than their first forbidden kisses had been, in stolen moments at the front alcove or in the ballroom, where anyone might have seen them.

Here, they were certain not to be interrupted. There was nothing more dangerous than that.

He propped himself up on one elbow—likely to allow her to breathe, or to voice concern about impropriety and a gentleman's disinclination to take advantage of a lady—but Dahlia loved having to gasp for air between breathtaking kisses. She didn't want propriety. She wanted Simon Spaulding. And she had him precisely where she wished: legs tangled with hers in the middle of her bed.

She reached up to loosen his cravat. If he intended

to ruin the moment with concessions to ladylike decorum, she'd yank him back down with his own strip of
linen and kiss him until gentlemanly behavior was the
last thing on his mind.

The moment the knot of his cravat loosened, Simon
ripped it from his throat and hauled Dahlia into his lap.

His kisses were faster than before, more demanding,
as his fingers unfastened the first of her shirt buttons
then flew back to his own shirt to unbutton his.

She met him kiss for kiss, her fingers tangling with
his as she fumbled free his shirt buttons while he unfastened hers.

He shucked his coat, his waistcoat, his shirt, then
paused as he reached for hers.

She lifted her arms over her head and arched her
back, silently challenging him to yank the thin cambric
over her head with the same mercilessness he'd treated
his own.

Rather than do so, he lifted the hem gently, slowly,
taking care to allow the ridges of his fingers to graze her
hips, her waist, her ribs, the sides of her breasts. Gooseflesh followed the trail of his touch, as did a growing
pool of desire that left every inch of her exposed skin
tingling in anticipation of his next touch.

When at last her shirt sailed over his broad shoulders
to join the other discarded garments upon the floor,
Dahlia's pulse beat so frantically she was certain he could
hear it. Her breasts were fuller than before, her nipples

hard and aching.

He tipped her backwards into the pillows, then lowered his mouth to hers.

"I've never undressed a woman in trousers before," he said gruffly. "I suppose there's a first time for everything."

Before she could think of an appropriate reply, he began a trail of incendiary kisses from her collarbone to the valley between her breasts, then down toward her waistline.

"I've never been stripped of my trousers before," she countered belatedly, and gasped as he accompanied each newly unbuttoned inch with a kiss or flick of his tongue to her bare flesh.

She tilted her pelvis to help him tug her gaping trousers down over her hips. He took advantage of the closer proximity and slid his tongue between her legs to touch her core. Her eyes rolled back in shock and pleasure.

He had not stripped her of her trousers as she had anticipated. He had left them bunched about her ankles, affording her just enough resistance to feel trapped, and yet more than enough freedom to widen her knees to give him greater access.

The twin sensation of being simultaneously submissive and demanding stole her breath and made every lick, every touch, all the more pleasurable. She had imagined being helpless in his arms. This was infinitely better. She could thread her fingers into his dark hair and force him even closer to her core, or she could widen her trembling legs and let him plunder her however he saw fit.

She cupped her hands over her breasts, capturing the stiff nipples between her fingers. Her body was no stranger to her own touch. Many nights when she thought of Simon, she placed her fingers where she thought he might touch, pinched where she thought he might pinch, rubbed where she thought he might rub.

But he didn't *know* she did that. Didn't know she'd had her fingers exactly where his tongue now licked. Didn't know how many delicious nights she'd teased her own nipples, pretending it was his hands, his mouth on her flesh, not hers.

With her head lolling back against the pillows, she could not see him between her legs. Perhaps right now, even as he licked her into distraction, his dark blue eyes were watching her cup her own breasts, toy with her own nipples. Perhaps his hands were not on the bed, but reaching into his own trousers, pulling out his—

She gasped as one of his fingers slid into her core, impaling as he licked, coaxing as he suckled. Waves of pleasure shot through her, rocketing her past all conscious thought. Her hands fell limp to her sides as the spasms tightened her legs and curled her toes.

Only when he'd taken everything from her did he tug the bunched trousers free from her still-trembling legs and position his bare hips against hers.

"Tell me you want this," he demanded between kisses.

"You know the answer," she managed to gasp, her body flickering back to life at the sensation of his shaft gliding again and again along her slick core.

"*Say it.*" His voice was rough as gravel, the tip of his shaft pressing at her opening. "Say it if you want it."

She gave her hips a sudden tilt, forcing the tip to fully penetrate her. "Do it. Make love to me. Make me forget my own name."

Before she had even finished talking, he sank into her inch by inch until she was no longer certain whether she'd spoken aloud or if *Make me forget my own name* had been the last coherent thought she'd managed to form in her mind.

The pain was first. Sharper than expected, but gone just as quickly.

His strokes were long, gentle. He probably imagined the slow, deliberate slide a way of easing her into the process, but she had never wanted easy. She wanted *him*. She wanted him to surrender to the same helpless ecstasy he had given to her.

Already her body had warmed to this new invasion. The parts he had licked were still so sensitive that her nerves sprang back to life with every hedonistic brush of his body against hers. Each stroke brought dual pleasure.

"Do you like this?" he whispered as he drove within her.

"I love it," she managed to gasp in reply.

The pleasure robbed her mind of its ability to form words. All she could do was feel.

The strokes of his hard shaft inside her and the luscious friction on the outside were a combination so potent she could do little more than lock her legs about his hips and ride each breathtaking thrust.

"Simon," she whispered. "Simon, I'm going to—"

The spasms fractured within her, the pleasure multiplying as her helpless muscles clenched and released his thick shaft as it stroked deep within her.

He pumped faster and faster and then jerked out from between her legs to bury his bucking hips in a blanket.

When she lifted her head in question, he slung one of his beautifully muscled arms about her waist and tilted his exhausted face toward hers.

"It's not the order I planned to do things," he murmured once he'd caught his breath, "but you're definitely the one I planned to do it with. I always knew my first would be my last. I'm glad it was you."

Dahlia turned her shocked gaze up to her bedchamber ceiling in dawning horror.

Simon hadn't thought this was a heat-of-the-moment dalliance—he'd thought he was proposing marriage.

And she had just stolen his virginity.

Chapter 26

Simon's brain was soporific from sated pleasure. His arms were limp, his legs were limp, his—*ahem*. Everything had been quite the opposite of limp just a few moments earlier.

For being his first time performing that particular dance, he rather thought he'd acquitted himself quite satisfactorily. And if there was room for improvement, well, that his favorite way to interpret *until death do us part*. He and Dahlia could spend the next thirty years perfecting the art of giving and receiving pleasure.

Then again, he hadn't yet spoken the words. He'd meant to—*tried* to, in fact, repeatedly—but somewhere between reaching for the ring downstairs and reaching for his cock upstairs, he'd lost sight of the script and become distracted by what was happening on the mattress instead.

Now that they'd snuck the cart before the horse,

however, it was past time to put things to rights.

He pushed himself up on one elbow and smiled. "Darling?"

She closed her eyes.

He cleared his throat and frowned. He'd been hoping for at least a modicum of visual reciprocity. Then again, perhaps this way was easier for her.

"I realize I've bungled the order of events," he tried again, "but I'm hoping from now on, we can do things right."

She grimaced as if beset by a sudden toothache.

He soldiered on. "It would make me the happiest of men, if you would do me the honor of—"

"No."

The word was so soft, it was barely audible over the pounding of Simon's heart and the rushing in his ears, and yet no whispered syllable had ever been louder or more devastating.

His knee! He had failed to propose on one knee. He was indeed bollixing the whole thing.

He leapt off the bed and nearly smacked face-first into the wall when he realized his breeches were still somewhere about his ankles. Cursing silently, he yanked the buckskin back up to his hips and carefully buttoned the fall before dropping to one knee directly in front of Dahlia's field of vision.

If she were to open her eyes, that was.

"*My darling Dahlia,*" he said far more loudly than he

intended.

Her eyes flew open, took in his genuflecting posture, and snapped shut even tighter than before.

The knee wasn't working. The words weren't working. He was going to have to try harder.

He grabbed her hands and yanked her into a seating position without releasing her fingers. She couldn't ignore him now. They were practically holding hands. She was pale and stark naked, but he was still down on one knee, so perhaps this time his proposal would work.

"Marry me," he said, skipping over the flowery bits. Perhaps the *happiest of men* line had become *outré*.

She tugged at her hands.

He refused to let her go.

Her shoulders slumped. "I can't."

"Can't?" he repeated, baffled. "Are you already married?"

She shook her head. "Of course not."

"Are you *underage*?" he asked, recoiling in horror.

"No!" She jerked her hands free and rubbed at her face. "Simon, I can't marry you. I cannot."

"Of course you can," he stammered. "There's three weeks of banns, and if that's too rushed, we can have as long of an engagement as you desire."

"There's no point to an engagement," she said miserably. "We're not getting married."

"Listen," he said quickly, then paused when he realized he had never worked up a compelling speech to persuade her to his point of view. "I don't have a title loftier than 'Inspector' and I'm afraid I haven't a palace, but my home is truly quite pretty. Its only lack is that you aren't there to—"

"I don't even know where you live," she interrupted, reaching for her trousers. "And you are never there. *This* is my home. Bow Street is yours."

"Well," he stammered as he searched in vain for a rejoinder. "All right, that's not a bad point. But it's also not the only point. I like you, Dahlia. I've enjoyed every moment I have spent with you. Er, possibly excepting this one. You have a quick mind and a bottomless heart. I think your school is wonderful. I think *you* are wonderful. I like your earnestness and your empathy and your unpredictable nature. I don't want to change you from who you are. I'd just like you to also be my bride."

"You've no idea who I am," she said with a sigh. "You think you do, but headmistress-in-trousers is possibly the smallest part."

"No one is their job," he assured her. "Being an inspector isn't the sum total of my life either."

Except it had been. Right up until he met her. She had helped him become a complete person. And was now tearing his heart into tiny pieces. His throat tightened.

She pulled her shirt over her head without comment and began to methodically fasten the buttons.

His neck heated. He was still bare chested. Here he was, trying to be devoted and romantic, and he looked about as presentable as some vagabond drunk on Blue Ruin.

Simon yanked his wrinkled shirt on as elegantly as could be expected, then shoved his clammy hands through the arm holes of his waistcoat and the sleeves of his rumpled tailcoat.

Clearly Dahlia was unsure about him. He either needed to become a better man or prove to her he was already a good one. Thus far, luck had not been with him.

She moved toward the bedchamber door and twisted the key in the lock.

His opportunity was quickly dwindling.

"Are you afraid I'm asking only out of obligation, because of what we just did in your bed?" Simon pulled the ring from his waistcoat pocket and brandished it with shaking fingers. "Dahlia, look at me. I love you. I always meant to ask."

"I love you, too." She swallowed visibly, her eyes glossy. "The answer is still no. It will always be no. I'm sorry, Simon. I am resolute."

Her words slammed into his gut like cannon fire. That was that. He had failed.

He gave a stiff nod and dropped the ring back into his pocket. If *love* wasn't enough to sway her, he had nothing left to offer. He held his head as high as he was able, rolled back his shoulders, and marched out of her bedchamber...

And out of her life for good.

Chapter 27

Dahlia sobbed into Simon's cravat.

She'd hurt him so badly he had stalked out without it—and now it was the only part of him she would ever have.

It still smelled like him. Six long days had passed of her draping it over her pillow at night in order to fall asleep with his scent on her skin, yet rest continued to elude her.

When she'd first realized that their passionate kisses verged on becoming an out-and-out affair, she'd assumed a single night's dalliance was something they both would welcome. On her end, grasping at *one night for love* straws had helped her grapple with the idea of being forced to wed for money or never marrying at all. On Simon's end...

God save her. She hadn't realized she'd be taking the man's virginity!

Dahlia buried her face in her hands and moaned. "I'm a *rake*."

The idea was both ludicrous and undeniable. She had knowingly and willfully engaged in sexual misconduct with an innocent party without inquiring into matters such as virginity, or having any intention of making an honest gentleman out of him.

It was the very definition of dishonorable behavior. She was as shameless a rakish scoundrel as any of the charming blackguards prowling the debutantes of the ton.

And she'd done it to the man she loved.

Of course she couldn't stop thinking about him. If that had been the case before she'd robbed him of his innocence, her guilt and obsession were tenfold now.

The problem with Simon was that he was too perfect. He felt as passionately about her as he did about upholding the law. What he didn't realize was that those two things were mutually exclusive. She loved him too much to marry him without him knowing the truth.

And if *did* learn the truth... he wouldn't marry her.

Her stalwart, ethical Simon held no tolerance whatsoever for crime of any kind, regardless of motive. His calling was that of inspector. He meted justice. He upheld the law. And he'd be the most celebrated lead inspector in all of London just as soon as he locked Dahlia up for her crimes.

She wished being "good" for him was a choice. If

only it were as simple as that! But no matter how carefully she minded her Ps, Qs, and petty larceny in the
future, she could not undo the hard choices she'd had to
make in the past.

Worse, the unvarnished truth was that she had no
idea what the future held. While she certainly *hoped* she
would never be sent to the gallows for a public execution
of the Thief of Mayfair, could she truly swear that she
wouldn't steal another broach or nick a pair of cufflinks
if pawning such items meant the safe return to their
owners and a speck of nutrition in the bellies of hungry
children?

Starving girls and boys died in London's rookeries
every single day. Dahlia refused to let her students be
one of them. She couldn't save every six-year-old chim-
neysweep or the pretty orphans "adopted" by brothel
madams. But she could bloody well make certain the two
dozen pupils in the St. Giles School for Girls never again
had to contemplate such a fate.

Molly, Louisa, Beatrice… every one of the children
counted on Dahlia to keep them safe. She was more than
a headmistress. She was a mother figure. She was family.

And, if need be, she was Robin Hood.

She knew the risks. But the needs of one never outweighed the needs of many. If risking her future meant
securing twenty-four others, then she was not sorry for
having done so. Not when it was the only way to give
these girls their best chance. Dahlia possessed many

faults, but she believed her greatest strength was her willingness to sacrifice everything for those she loved.

Simon, on the other hand, felt differently. This was not a character defect on his part so much as a difference in philosophy. While Dahlia believed in creating the greatest amount of good for the greatest amount of people, Simon…believed in the law.

The law wasn't bad. Dahlia liked the law. In fact, if it were upheld a little more frequently in the rookeries, none of her girls would have been in the horrible situations she'd rescued them from.

The problem with the law was the lawlessness of it. If one had a title, one could worry significantly less about the law. If one had money, the same privilege applied. If one lived in a rookery or in abject poverty, the law was unlikely to show its face. If one lived far enough away from a magistrate or a watchman, it was as if those things had never existed at all.

Simon was not blind to these failings. His belief in the law was because he needed it to start working. He knew firsthand what it was like to be beneath the law's notice, had witnessed titles and gold bend rules past the breaking point. Those things hadn't disillusioned him. They'd made him stronger. He'd chosen to *be* the change he wished to see in the world.

He was a good man. An honest inspector. A force of nature and a source of positive change in Bow Street and everywhere his horse took him. The world was very much the richer for having a man like Inspector Spaulding looking after it.

She could never tell him what she'd done. Nor could she promise to stop doing it.

Which meant they could never be together.

A knock sounded on the bedchamber door. "Dahlia? Are you ready for dance lessons?"

Faith. It was past time to tell her.

Dahlia shoved the tearstained cravat beneath her pillow and cracked open the door.

"No lessons." She pushed her damp hair from her face. "Mr. Spaulding has resigned his position."

Faith's mouth fell open in shock. "What happened?"

"Nothing," Dahlia said quickly, forcing a wobbly smile. "We wanted different things."

"That. Contemptible. *Pig.*" Understanding flashed across Faith's face. She pulled Dahlia into a fierce hug.

"I'm the pig," Dahlia mumbled into her best friend's shoulder. "It's not like your situation at all. He wanted to marry me. I had to say no." The school was most important, she reminded herself to beat back the stinging in her eyes and the breaking of her heart. "He's a good man. He'll find someone better."

"*No* one is a better person that you," Faith said through clenched teeth. "I have never met anyone as kindhearted or loyal. I can't imagine him finding a better match than you."

That was likely because Faith didn't quite realize the

lines that had been crossed in order to keep the school afloat.

It might not change her assessment of Dahlia being kindhearted and loyal, but as to Simon never finding a better match... Well. Surely there was a young lady out there whose hanging wouldn't give him a promotion.

Faith leaned back, her hands still on Dahlia's shoulders. "Do you want me to tell the students?"

Dahlia shook her head. "I'll go with you."

"Not like that." Faith's expression contorted. "You look terrible."

"You're a true friend," Dahlia muttered as she turned to look for the washbasin.

"I'll just tell them," Faith offered. "Your face will be splotchy for a while."

Dahlia set down her washrag with a sigh. Faith was probably right. "Are they already in the ballroom?"

Faith's eyes lit up. "The schoolroom. You should see how excited they get when they realize they can sound out words! What we really need are enough primers so that every girl can have her own."

"I know." Dahlia splashed water onto her face to hide her sigh of failure.

"Didn't you say you were going to bring a few old books from your childhood nursery?" Faith asked. "It's not the same as every student with the same primer, but having more than three dilapidated books in our schoolroom would make a huge difference for the girls."

"I did say that," Dahlia agreed without turning around. "Something came up."

Something like rent being due and no way to pay it. She'd had to pawn every book in her childhood library along with her pearl combs and her umbrella, but she had managed to settle every one of their overdue accounts.

Until next month, anyway.

Faith patted her shoulder. "Just let me know if you find a book or two for the girls. I'll be happy to add it to the curriculum."

Dahlia nodded. "You'll be the first one I tell."

As soon as Faith left, Dahlia closed the door and slumped her shoulders against the nearest wall.

This was why she couldn't have Simon. What she wanted was not as important as what she could do for others.

No matter how her heart might break.

Chapter 28

The last thing Dahlia was in the mood for was an evening of husband-hunting, perpetrated by her mother.

However, this, much like many things lately, was not up to Dahlia. She could not afford to pass up any opportunity to raise money for her school—and this time, she had an offer the love-to-be-scandalized ton could not refuse.

"It's called Circus Minimus," she explained at the fourth soirée that evening. This one was hosted by Lady Pettibone, although the Old Dragon was fortunately nowhere to be seen. "You've all been to Astley's and seen the professional acrobats and horse-masters. What you haven't seen is a performance by two dozen schoolgirls whose tumbling feats will cause just as much awe."

Lady Upchurch raised a skeptical brow. "How can anyone perform tumbling feats in stays and a day dress?"

"They can't," Dahlia said simply, delighted at how

easily bored society wives continued to walk into her trap. "They'll be wearing cambric shirts and boys' trousers, of course."

"Trousers!" Lady Upchurch gasped, sending a shocked glance over her shoulder at the other fashionable ladies. "I couldn't possibly condone such a scandalous event."

"But when is it?" asked Mrs. Epworth with a sparkle in her eyes. "Just in case a few of us feel like…temporarily condoning."

Dahlia tried to hide her grin. "Circus Minimus will be performed one week from Saturday at the St. Giles School for Girls. Seats are not cheap, and will be first come, first served. Two p.m. sharp, mind you."

"First come, first served!" Lady Roundtree harrumphed in privileged disdain. "Surely there is *some* way to reserve one's place in advance. I know you cannot expect viscounts and earls to queue outside a schoolhouse as if they were back at Eton."

Lady Roundtree's husband was neither a viscount nor an earl, but rather a humble baron, just like Dahlia's father. And as such, Dahlia had been counting on precisely this response.

"Well," she drew out slowly, as if the idea were only just now occurring to her. "I really oughtn't to play favorites, as it isn't at all fair to the other ladies. But I suppose I could reserve the front row for whichever patrons make the highest donation to the school. We could even put plaques in the library bearing those patrons' names. I do imagine the society pages will be quite lively, come Sunday morning. Especially since the audience will be so exclusive."

Lady Roundtree snapped open her reticule. "How much?"

"She said *highest donation*, Mabel, not 'pin money under your handkerchief," Lady Upchurch snapped. "If I were to speak to my solicitor, when would the school need to receive the donation?"

"Next Friday, at the latest." Dahlia widened her eyes innocently. "It would be far too embarrassing to leave it a surprise, and have some poor souls discover they haven't a seat waiting for them after all."

"Indeed." Lady Roundtree shivered. "Can you imagine such horror?"

Pride warmed Dahlia's chest. Thanks to Faith, she had been able to come up with a brilliant idea to raise funds for the school—and extort the highest amount of donations possible in the process—but it was her girls who would be putting on the actual performance.

They had spent the past month dedicated to their tumbling practice. Some were better than others at turning somersaults, and a few were more suited to playing "horse" than leaping riding-master, but every one of them had spent countless hours drilling acrobatic routines on the ballroom rug until they could perform their roles in their sleep.

She had every reason to be proud of her girls. With

luck, a quarterly showing would generate enough funds to keep the school afloat.

Until the performance, however... Dahlia would have to come up with *something* to keep the creditors at bay. Their knocks had become more insistent. She needed to come up with money soon. Perhaps there would be more charitable ladies at the next soiree.

If not... Dahlia wasn't sure *what* she would do.

She excused herself from the group of ladies and headed toward the refreshment table in search of her mother. Grenville ladies never strayed far from the closest ratafia pitcher.

Blocking her way, however, was none other than Lady Pettibone. Almack's patroness. Sister to a duke. Hostess of tonight's soirée.

Dahlia pasted a smile on her face. "Thank you for a lovely party."

The cold fire in Lady Pettibone's eyes could have smote an entire village.

"Are you blind?" she asked, her voice high and brittle. "Do you not see that I am speaking with my friends?"

"I-I was just asking a question," Mrs. Kingsley stammered. "We don't need to keep talking about your library."

The infamous Pettibone library. Dahlia resisted the urge to roll her eyes.

Books are for looks was Lady Pettibone's alleged motto, although no one of Dahlia's acquaintance could

actually corroborate the existence of the famed Pettibone library. Spines that had never been broken. Pages
that had never been cut. Words that would never be
read, because extensive libraries were for symbolizing
one's social status, not for personal improvement.

"As I was saying," Lady Pettibone enunciated pointedly. "I have never so much as touched the illustrated
etchings. I am morally against such salacious content.
Unfortunately, my dear, such a vast collection is simply
too expensive to destroy. One must be practical above
all things, I always say. Practical and humble."

The irony…it burned. *Books are for boasting* might as
well have been the motto. Dahlia wasn't sure how much
longer she'd be able to stop herself from rolling her eyes.

"Is your library here in this townhouse?" Miss
Willoughby asked.

"A small selection." Lady Pettibone sniffed. "It
takes up the entire next floor. I must walk up two flights
to my retiring quarters, but we all must make sacrifices."

Dahlia wouldn't mind showing her what sacrifice
truly meant. If she wasn't going to allow anyone to read
her books, she might as well set them on fire.

"Have you any children's primers?" she found herself asking.

"Oh, have I." Lady Pettibone laughed. "I have an
uncut collection of every set in existence. Two, in some
cases. They give one such nostalgic pleasure, wouldn't
you say?"

"Have you gifted any to nieces or nephews?" asked Mrs. Kingsley. "I have loved books since I was a child."

"My copies are *uncut*," Lady Pettibone enunciated pointedly, "and *expensive*. They would be neither of those things if I allowed children to put their grubby hands on them."

Dahlia heroically refrained from drowning Lady Pettibone in the ratafia bowl.

She couldn't afford allowing a smart retort to alienate future donations from the other ladies in attendance. But it sounded like she could afford almost anything if she could get her hands on just one of the picture-perfect books turning to dust in Lady Pettibone's library.

Chapter 29

If Dahlia had learned anything after her near-disaster at Phineas Mapleton's house, it was that sneaking back inside after the guests had gone home erased all hope of deniability. As well as opened up an entire host of new complications.

Being caught on the wrong floor while the festivities were still underway, however, left more options open. She might have a bad sense of direction. She might have a wicked megrim and need to lie down. Actually, *yes*. That was the perfect excuse. Especially now that she knew the bedchambers—including the guest quarters—were on the floor above the library.

If she just happened to pass through on her way to an emergency lie-down, one could hardly find evil in that, could they?

The first trick had been convincing her mother to

go on ahead to the next party. This had been accomplished by Dahlia insisting she needed to ride with an old friend in order to catch up on past news in the carriage. And by promising to consider some gentleman her mother had dug up, who professed a willingness to entertain the idea of allowing his wife to run a charity from afar...so long as it benefitted the right kind of people. Obviously a school for indigents wouldn't do.

Dahlia would rather stab herself in the eye than be trapped in a thirty-minute waltz with a paragon like that.

The second step had been actually going to the second floor and spending an hour writhing on a fainting couch until one of the maids chanced upon her.

Dahlia hadn't given her name, but she'd mentioned the phantom megrim and heavily implied that Lady Pettibone had kindly offered the use of her guest chambers to any soul in need.

Plan A was not getting caught. Plan B was setting up her innocence.

After the maid left, Dahlia waited another hour before sneaking back down to the library. The twilight hour between when a party was winding down and when the guests had actually left was the perfect time to be somewhere one wasn't expected. The carriages would be queueing out front. Lady Pettibone would be bidding her adieus.

Dahlia would nicking an expensive reading primer.

She tiptoed down the marble staircase and slipped through the library door. Her mouth fell open at the sea of shelves that awaited her.

Row after row of books covered every surface from floor to vaulted ceiling. Twin balconies flanked each side of the long hall, accessible only via a mahogany ladder with thick black wheels at the base of one balcony.

Dahlia stared up at those mouthwatering, out-of-reach shelves. She *knew* she should grab the closest book and go. Of course she knew it. But those out of reach books could only be one thing: Lady Pettibone's collection of too-shocking-to-glimpse illustrated etching.

Not only was Dahlia filled with a sudden urge to flip through every one of those pages, those tomes were inherently far more valuable.

Even if the one she grabbed didn't turn out to be one-of-a-kind or of unique literary merit, it would still be a salacious etching. Any pawnbroker in London would be more than happy to take an item like that off her hands. No matter what price she set, the pawnbroker would double his investment by teatime.

How many boxes of cheap used books might she purchase with the sale of a single such tome? How many pinafores, and pairs of shoes, and tallow candles, and bars of soap, and loaves of bread?

She was up the ladder before her mind could finish calculating sums.

The top row of books was mildly titillating. Depicted therein were more than a few acts she'd imagined performing with her favorite inspector. The bottom row, however, contained scenes so shocking that the first book she opened fell from her fingers to the floor.

She froze. The book had only fallen a few inches. No harm had come. The balcony's carpeted landing had both muffled the sound and protected the book from injury. She herself was hidden from view, crouched as she was between the balcony's twin shelves.

And yet something didn't feel quite right.

A creak in one of the center floorboards indicated she was no longer alone in the library.

Her heart skipped, then doubled its furious pace.

Who could be down there? A servant? Another guest? Lady Pettibone? Nothing more than Dahlia's overactive imagination?

Another floorboard creaked. Slowly. Methodically.

Whoever was down there was making the rounds of the entire library. Walking the perimeter. Checking each aisle.

Checking for *what?* Dahlia clutched the pocket-sized book of etchings to her thudding chest. Looking for *her?*

The footsteps plodded through the maze of shelves and came to rest right beneath her small balcony.

Dahlia was too scared to move, every shaking limb frozen in fear.

As she watched in panic, the mahogany ladder resting against her balcony rail began to roll along its oiled track until it reached the opposite balcony on the other side of the open hall.

Thirty feet of empty air stretched between the end

of her railing and the first rung of the ladder.

It might as well be an ocean.

Please don't climb up the ladder, she repeated in her mind. *Please don't climb up the ladder. Please don't find me. Please go away.*

After a long, excruciating moment, the footsteps retreated from the balcony and made their way through the maze of shelves to the exit at the front of the room.

The library was safe.

Dahlia still didn't dare breathe. Her limbs trembled too much to withstand her weight. Sliding one of her half-boots forward so much as an inch sent a wave of pins-and-needles up her cramping legs so painful she thought she would scream.

She did not scream. She was too panicked to scream. Whoever had come to check the library could return at any moment. She had to get out. She had to get out *now*.

Dahlia pushed to her feet despite the fiery pain rippling up her numb legs from crouching too long on the floor. She could massage her over-exerted muscles later.

Right now, she had to find a way out.

Flying across the library to the ladder on the opposite balcony was out of the question. As was leaping from her railing to one of the freestanding bookshelves. With her luck, the force of her landing would push it off balance and each mahogany bookshelf would knock into the other like the most expensive set of library dominoes on the planet.

Her only choice was to drop down twelve feet to the Axminster carpet below and pray she didn't break an ankle in the process.

The next question was how.

She shoved the little book of etchings into her bosom behind her fichu and reached down to gather her hems. There was no practical way of climbing the railing without flashing her bare buttocks to the entire world, but waiting for Lady Pettibone to stumble upon her was hardly a better option.

This was tumbling, she told herself. She'd done far more dangerous acrobatics with her brother Heath as a child. To be sure, they hadn't involved her vaulting bare-arsed over the railing of a high society balcony. Heath had no doubt had to vault over his fair share of balconies in his time. Why not Dahlia?

This would simply become a funny story to tell her brother someday over lemon cakes.

She scooped up her skirts and hiked her legs up onto the balcony railing.

Please don't break, she begged in her mind. *Please don't break loose before I can let go and float safely to the carpet below.*

With a deep breath, she launched herself off the railing, twisting so that her back would take the brunt of the fall.

It wasn't going to work. Her legs went one way. The book flew another.

Every bone was about to—

A pair of warm, strong arms caught her before she

could crash to the library floor. Warm, strong arms that should not have been anywhere near there. She'd heard the footsteps *exit*, blast it all. Silently doubling back to catch a criminal red-handed was the worst kind of deductive brilliance. The sort that meant she'd fallen straight into the arms of celebrated Bow Street Runner, Inspector Simon Spaulding.

Who was finally due that promotion.

Chapter 30

Simon's heart went cold.

He had quite literally *caught* the Thief of Mayfair in his arms—and the two-faced criminal was none other than headmistress Dahlia Grenville.

Ex-headmistress.

He dropped her unceremoniously onto the expensive, high society carpet.

As she fell, a palm-sized leather-bound book had popped out of her bodice, along with a scrap of lace apparently meant to keep both bosoms and contraband safely out of sight.

He nudged the expensive leather volume with the toe of his boot.

She winced and covered her eyes.

Simon did not. His were finally open. And he could not have felt more betrayed.

Dahlia was not who he'd thought she was. He'd

been shocked to glimpse her hobnobbing with aristocrats. Not waiting on them as a servant, or even rubbing
shoulders on accident, going about the duties of an honest, hardworking boarding school administrator.

No, she'd been swanning about in a gown so exquis-
ite it hurt the eyes. Laughing with this duchess or that
countess as if they were old friends. Because they *were*.

She had never been part of Simon's world. She'd
been born into another plane. One of champagne and
hors d'œuvres, diamonds and pearls, lady's maids and
liverymen whose daily uniforms cost more than Simon's
annual salary. Dahlia was far from the hard-luck, working-class angel he'd believed her to be.

She was a liar. A hypocrite. A beautiful, mercenary,
Janus-faced thief.

He'd never known her at all.

"Get up," he growled.

She leapt to her feet with the agility of an acrobat.
Or the grace of a debutante with a private dancing-master and expensive finishing school.

Or the habits of a well-practiced thief.

"Why are you here?" she stammered, with a glance
over her shoulder. "Did you follow me?"

"I was hunting the Thief of Mayfair," he said coldly.
"So, yes. It appears I followed you."

Her cheeks flushed. "But how did you know I'd be
here?"

"I didn't have to," he said simply. "The Thief of

Mayfair targets wealthy aristocrats, either during or shortly after a showy gathering. Once I compiled a list of upcoming ton parties, it was easy to determine which hosts had items of great value within easy reach. Those individuals tend to share that information with the entire world."

Dahlia lowered her head. "Lady Pettibone paid you to guard her library?"

"That would be unethical." Simon flashed a hard smile. "The government already pays me to investigate crimes and protect its citizens. What kind of monster would I be to accept money I didn't deserve?"

She swallowed visibly. "Simon, I—"

"No need to explain," he said icily. "I know what you are. I observed you in your natural environment."

"You... saw me with the other ladies?" she guessed hopefully.

"Believe me. Your ratafia consumption is the least of my concerns." Stuffing expensive objects into her bodice was quite another. There was no denying the evidence.

Dahlia was a thief.

His heart hardened as he plucked the fallen book from the ground.

"It isn't mine," she blurted.

He slid her a flat look. "Obviously."

"That doesn't mean I was stealing it," she said quickly. But her face had drained of color.

"Doesn't it?" he said in bored tones.

"Or that I'm the Thief of Mayfair," she added.

"Aren't you?"

"I..." She rolled back her shoulders. "I was forced to lie down in the guest quarters due to a megrim."

"Ill-timed, I'm sure," he murmured.

"Ask the maids," she insisted. "They saw me. When I had recovered enough to return to the party, I passed through the library and simply lost track of time."

"For two hours." He didn't bother to hide his skepticism.

"It's...a good library," she mumbled.

"It's off limits," he corrected firmly. "Lady Pettibone told you so personally."

Dahlia cringed. "You heard her say that?"

"She tells everyone. Lying to me doesn't change facts." He held up the book. "You broke in to steal from her."

"I didn't break in," Dahlia hedged.

"But you do steal. You've done so all season." He curled his lip. "The signs were there. I just didn't want to see them."

She winced. "There were signs I was a thief?"

"Signs you were an...unusual headmistress," he allowed. "I thought it was charming at first."

"Did you?" She raised her lashes to stare at him.

It no longer mattered. He crossed his arms. "If I search the school, will I find the stolen objects?"

"Only if you look in the schoolroom." She leaned

forward in defiance. "Pocket globes and a trio of disintegrating reading primers are the sum total of our educational materials."

"That doesn't make stealing right."

"Does it make it wrong?" Her gaze turned pleading. "All the objects were returned to their rightful owners."

"Except the pocket globes," he pointed out.

"Mapleton's a special case," she muttered. "I'm half-surprised one of his competition hasn't stomped on his collection long ago."

Frankly, so was Simon. The man was a slug. But it didn't change facts.

He hardened his voice toward Dahlia. "You have to give them back."

And he had to turn her in.

She sent another furtive glance over her shoulder. "Where is everyone? Aren't you going to parade me in front of Lady Pettibone?"

"I shall parade you inside the Magistrates' Court," he promised. "Lady Pettibone took her post-party laudanum, and there is no need to wake her."

Hope entered Dahlia's eyes for the first time since she'd fallen into his arms. "So, right now...nobody knows but us?"

Simon raised a brow.

He knew what she was asking. As things stood, they could both walk away. No one would know...but Simon. Except it was his job to ensure such travesties of justice never happened.

No. More than that. It was Simon's mission. The driving force that had given his life meaning ever since his parents' death at the hands of a highwayman. A highwayman who had never been caught.

But what if he had? What if months or weeks earlier, some soft-hearted imbecile had agreed to give the blackguard a second chance? That was somehow worse than Simon's long held belief that the highwayman had simply managed to evade capture.

One lazy watchman, one corrupt magistrate, one irresponsible investigator was all it took to put others' lives and property at risk. Simon had sworn never to be one of them. Had held his head high for three ethical decades that would make any man proud. But he hadn't done it for himself, or even to avenge the death of his mother. He did it because it was the right thing to do. All people deserved to be treated fairly. By their contemporaries—and in the eyes of the law.

Which meant there was no choice here. Not for him, and not for Dahlia. A thief was a thief. And crime had to pay.

Even if it meant sending the love of his life to Newgate.

He tried to swallow the ball of anger and betrayal clogging his throat.

To say he was disappointed in her would be a laughable understatement. He'd believed in her goodness. Wanted to *marry* her, for the love of God. Had possessed absolute, wholehearted faith that she was precisely the sort of woman that would make any Bow Street inspector proud.

And everything about her was a lie.

Until recently, he'd believed all his dreams would come true if only he could earn a coveted promotion by catching the Thief of Mayfair. Turned out, the villain was his would-be fiancée. Whose big brown eyes were glassy with unshed tears because the man she'd refused to marry was the only one who could save her from the gallows.

It was no longer about his career, or his promotion. Turning her in meant ruining her life. Even prisoners who weren't sentenced to hang never lasted long in the squalid, disease-filled prisons.

Yet he'd sworn an oath to do the right thing, even when it was hard. *Especially* when it was hard. The hardest thing he'd ever have to do in his life.

"Simon?" she said, her eyes and voice pleading.

He pulled out his iron handcuffs and snapped them onto her wrists.

Chapter 31

Dahlia watched behind blurry eyes as the man she loved tethered a sturdy rope from the saddle of his horse to her handcuffs.

It wasn't Simon's fault. It was hers. Simon's tireless determination and strength to uphold both his values and the law no matter the opposition was one of the main reasons she'd fallen in love with him in the first place. He could be counted on to always do the right thing. He was her rock. A bastion of unbreakable character.

Whose unflagging heroic qualities were now marching her to a dire future of her own making.

She was going to lose everything. Life as she knew it. Her school. Her family. Her lifelong friendship with Faith. From this day forward, the iron shackles about her wrists would be her sole companions.

And her girls… What would they think? What

would they *do?*

Faith would not be able to manage the school alone. Without Dahlia's aid, donations would be minimal. The girls might be evicted from the abbey before they even had a chance to attempt the fund-raising performance.

A chill skittered across her clammy skin. She could not consign her wards back to a life on the streets. There had to be something she could do.

She turned her panicked gaze toward Simon. "Please set me free. I won't do it again."

"I know." He swung onto his horse. "You'll be in prison."

The chill from the heavy iron cuffs seeped all the way through to her bones.

Once she stepped foot into prison, she was as good as dead. Either the gallows or gaol fever would take her.

Even if she somehow convinced Simon to let her go, just this once… to forget he'd caught her in the library, forget that her schoolroom contained pocket-sized proof of her past crimes as a thief… Her days of playing Robin Hood were over.

If she couldn't pay the rent, her school—the family of girls who counted on her, looked up to her, loved her—were right back on the streets.

Just like they were when their birth mothers abandoned them.

Was it better to have loved and lost? Or had she only made things worse for them all?

The iron shackles clinked as she clutched her suddenly nauseous belly.

If there had been any other way... but, of course, there hadn't. If Dahlia hadn't taken the risks she had, they would have run out of bread to eat long before. Creditors would have evicted them from the abbey. If she weren't facing a Newgate prison sentence, it would be debtors' gaol at Marshalsea. Ending like this had always been inevitable.

She just hoped her girls could forgive her.

With her new notoriety, she was likely to be the sole member of the ton to miss the upcoming Circus Minimus. Fashionable quarterly performances were no longer likely. This would be the girls' one shot. They would no longer be students of perennial interest, but a flash-in-the-pan passing fancy, like the "penny freaks" of a traveling peep tent.

Everyone would want to see the school where the duplicitous Dahlia Grenville had worked before being locked up at Newgate.

And then "everyone" would go home, thrilled to see themselves listed as attending guests in the scandal columns, and forget all about the two dozen child performers from that day forward.

Dahlia's chest grew tight. She wasn't just disappointing her wards. She was abandoning them. They would go back to the workhouses, the brothels, the streets. Because of her, the children could lose the only family they'd ever had.

She had to find a way to save them.

But how? Every cobblestone she tripped over only brought her closer and closer to gaol.

There had to be something. Anything. No matter how small. She had to think, despite the pounding in her head and the bleakness in her heart. The dank, offal-stained air of a long, black alley might be the last breaths of freedom she ever had. Her girls deserved her full attention now more than ever. She was still their only hope.

Or was she? Dahlia's cracked lips parted.

Although nothing was likely to lift the school above the stigma of the previous felonious headmistress, with luck, the Circus Minimus would garner enough donations to stay ahead of the bill collectors for another month or two.

If anyone could find a way to keep the school open until the performance, it would be Faith. But to even attempt it, she would need *some* buffer of time and money.

As well as legal authorization.

"Stop," Dahlia choked out as she stumbled along the alley.

The school was her dream. The last thing she wanted to do was give it up. But she'd left herself—and her students—no choice.

Simon didn't slow. "You'll have plenty opportunity to rest once you're locked inside a cell."

"*Please*," she begged, hobbling faster to reach his

side. "Let me pen a short note to my brother before you take me in."

"Why?"

"He has a document signed by me, handing all ownership and control of the school over to Faith Digby in the event I am no longer capable of doing so." She lifted her shackled wrists and tried for a brave smile. "I assume hanging from the gallows isn't a holiday one ever returns from. It's the only thing I can do to take care of my girls."

Chapter 32

Simon stopped his horse.

His life had taken on an unreal quality. It was well past midnight on a starless night. He was leading his horse in a slow, mile-and-a-half trek down dark, empty alleyways from Mayfair to Bow Street. Whilst dragging along in iron cuffs the woman he'd hoped would be his bride.

"I'm going to unshackle you," he said. "But only because it's faster for you to ride up here with me."

She nodded quickly. "May I send a message to my brother when we reach the court?"

Probably. Allowing her to pen a letter would break protocols, not laws. Although he had no choice but to arrest Dahlia, Simon would do everything in his power to minimize the damage her arrest could inflict on her wards.

He slid from his horse and fished the keys from the

saddle pocket.

Part of him still couldn't quite believe the events that were unfolding. This was *Dahlia*. And he'd shackled her like a common thief.

She *was* a common thief, he reminded himself firmly as he slipped the key into the iron lock. An *un*common thief, perhaps, but still a thief. Nothing was happening tonight that she couldn't have prevented herself. He was not the villain. This was not his fault.

When the iron cuffs fell away, white skin rubbed raw from constant contact with the heavy metal was visible even in the half-light of a crescent moon.

He was *not* the villain, Simon reminded himself. He was *not*.

"Why did you do this?" he asked her softly. "What made you think you could talk your way out of a conviction?"

She hesitated before answering. "I'm a baron and baroness's daughter. I thought—"

He dropped her hands.

"You thought what?" he demanded, his laugh harsh and unmusical. "Having titled blood makes you exempt from the law? I'm the son of a marquess and roses have never flown out my arse. If I commit a crime, I fully expect to go to prison like I'd deserve."

Even as he said the words, he realized the comparison was invalid. For all that a marquess outranked a mere baron, Simon was a bastard and Dahlia was legitimate.

Of course she was spoilt and self-indulgent. She'd been raised to be from birth.

"It doesn't matter who your father is," he bit out. "You are no lady. You're nothing but a thief."

She made no objection to this pronouncement.

He wished that made him feel better.

The truth was, she was far more than a thief. Far more than a baroness's daughter, even if her peers didn't notice. Simon did. He had witnessed the fierceness with which she protected her flock the very moment he'd met her. She'd brained a footpad with a broom, just to keep him away from a total stranger.

A total stranger who now looked up to Dahlia as if she'd hung the sun and moon.

The students worshiped her because she was their hero, their mentor, and their mother, all wrapped into one. They didn't love her because her parents were titled. They didn't even know.

Simon hadn't known either.

She might have mentioned that tiny fact at any point during their short-lived courtship. If not over the dinner table, then at least in Lady Pettibone's library. *I should get away with it because of my noble birth* had proven for centuries to be far more persuasive than *I should get away with it due to my noble intentions.*

The only logical reason she might have had for failing to mention her highborn connections at every ·turn…was that she hadn't wished to use them. It seemed she had wished to make her own way. Just like Simon or anyone else. Dahlia wanted to be judged not by her father's title, but rather by her own actions.

And now, unfortunately, she would.

Her parents might be titled, but Dahlia was not. And between the two of them, Simon was the one with the power. From the moment he filed his report, her life would be over.

He lifted her onto his horse. Her shoulders caved inward, and she remained as motionless and lifeless as a rag doll.

She didn't look like the daughter of a baron. She looked like a defeated, heartbroken young woman being sent away from everything and everyone she ever loved.

He rubbed the back of his neck. There was one more possible reason why Dahlia might have neglected to mention her position in society.

Which was that Dahlia didn't give two figs about her elevated position in society.

Why else would she be running a boarding school for indigent girls instead of a finishing school for debutantes? Come to think of it, why would she be performing philanthropic acts for those of a lower station at all?

Simon was the one who cared about class differences. He was the one obsessed with his younger brother, the marquess, and how Simon could never truly be a gentleman, thanks to his illegitimacy.

By reducing her to nothing more than the rank of

her parents, he was discounting her over the details of her birth the same way people had always discounted by-blows like him for the circumstances of theirs. Who was this woman, really?

He forced himself to meet her eyes.

"Will it help if I promise never to do it again?" she asked, when he didn't climb up behind her.

"No," he said with tired honesty. "The past cannot be changed."

But could it be forgiven?

Had she done anything that truly required his for-giveness? Would she want it anyway?

He swung himself up behind her and reached for the reins.

This was likely to be the last time he ever held her in his arms. Trapping her atop a horse bound for the Mag-istrates' Court was perhaps not the *most* romantic act one might perform when caught alone beneath the moon-light but, well, here they were.

The fancy raiment she currently wore looked noth-ing like the simple garments he was used to seeing her in, but the scent of her hair beneath his nose was the same as he remembered.

She smelled like waltzing lessons and stolen kisses. Circus balconies and dinners with friends. Laughter and lovemaking.

And now the scent would remind him of betrayal.

Hers, and his.

Dahlia was willing to sacrifice herself to help those

she loved at any cost. It was her greatest weakness and noblest strength. Those she loved, she loved completely and unconditionally. She would die to protect them. Love to her was worth far more than any personal gain.

As for Simon, what would he do? What did love mean to him?

He did have a choice, he realized. He would have to decide between the woman he loved and his very sense of self.

He'd become a Bow Street investigator to defend the weak. Avenge the forgotten. Protect the helpless.

Those were the same reasons why Dahlia had opened the St. Giles School for Girls. She had invested every penny she possessed, every hour in the day, every shred of her reputation into creating a better, safer world for those who could not.

She wasn't sorry. She didn't repent her crimes. If she discovered some way to smuggle crusts of stale bread from Newgate to St. Giles, he had no doubt she wouldn't hesitate to do so.

He covered the raw skin of her delicate wrists with his hand. Sometimes, doing the right thing caused a lot of wrong.

And somethings, doing the wrong thing caused a lot of right.

The students at Dahlia's school were desperate, poverty-stricken little girls just like his mother had been. When she'd made the leap from prostitute to courtesan, she'd believed fate was finally on her side. Instead, it had killed her.

How many times had he wondered what her life might have been like if she'd had the chance to follow a different path? Simon's mother had never been given the opportunity to find out. It might be too late for women like Simon's mother, but the twenty-four children at Dahlia's school could still be saved.

He stopped the horse. "Never again?"

Dahlia stiffened. "What?"

He gripped her arms. "You would promise? Even if it meant putting your school and your girls in jeopardy?"

"I would put them more in jeopardy by refusing to promise," she stammered. "I'll swear anything you want."

He slid off his horse so he could meet her eyes.

Her gaze was more wary than hopeful.

"It's not just a promise," he said softly. "It has to be true. If anyone finds out I've let a thief walk free, my career isn't just over. I'll be sent to Newgate, too."

"Nothing on this earth would make me risk your life for mine," she said without hesitation. "Losing you because of something I did… If you need to send me to the gallows, send me."

He lifted her hands. "Your girls need you more than I need a police commendation."

Her eyes widened. "What are you saying?"

"I'm saying no more risks," he said firmly. "Not now. Not ever."

She nodded. "I promise you, Simon. No more risks. I swear on my life."

Well…perhaps *one* more risk, he realized with a sigh. He did trust her. And knew she loved him as much as he loved her.

He was going to have to let a thief walk.

Chapter 33

Simon tried to focus on the case files cluttering his home study.

It was useless.

His once-legendary concentration and focus was now constantly fractured by the one criminal he'd decided not to chase.

Miss Dahlia Grenville.

His angst didn't solely stem from the dissonance of having committed the one act he'd sworn to never do. The world *was* gray, not black and white. She'd been right about that. Just like she was right that saving the lives of twenty-four children was more important than incarcerating for life the thief who had tried to rescue them.

Simon wasn't sorry he'd let Dahlia go. He was sorry the culprit was *Dahlia*.

In his mind, she and her school had been a much-needed safe zone. The one place he didn't have to worry about hunting felons. The one person he would never have to investigate. She was a soft-hearted headmistress with a penchant for exercising in men's trousers. Quirky, not criminal. With her, he could breathe in peace.

Except none of it was real.

She was all those things, but she wasn't *only* those things. Her Beau Monde parentage was the perfect disguise for her high society peers. Her benevolent employment in London's worst rookery had done the same for everyone else. Including him.

A low-class St. Giles headmistress would never have been allowed inside the fancy townhouses he'd been sent to investigate. She'd seemed exactly like the persona she'd presented herself as being. It was even true, as long as she was within the boarding school walls. When she stepped outside, however...

The brass knocker sounded from the front of his flat.

Simon tossed his files across his desk. He wasn't reading them anyway. He might as well torture himself with a long overdue conversation with the Thief of Mayfair.

Dahlia had sent a letter requesting an audience the very morning after the Pettibone debacle. For three days, Simon had ignored both her overture and her question. There was plenty to talk about, but first he'd needed to take the time to adjust.

He was unconvinced he'd succeeded.

With tight muscles, he opened his front door. "Dahlia."

"Simon." She hesitated at the threshold as if unsure he'd truly allow her in.

He still wasn't certain of its wisdom.

This morning, he had finally sent a reply. His home address. One o'clock in the afternoon.

Given the subject matter, meeting her at his Bow Street office was out of the question. Meeting at the school brought up too many memories. Too many pairs of curious eyes. Too many schoolgirls he'd already begun to miss. Lamentably, Simon's home was the most impersonal venue he could think of.

His flat would give them the privacy to finally be honest.

"Come in," he said at last.

She took a cautious step forward.

He was not of a humor to brew her a pot of tea, so he led her to the small parlor he was never home to use, rather than the dining area next to the kitchen.

"Your flat is quite airy and spacious," Dahlia commented in obvious surprise as she entered the sitting room. "Lots of windows. It's rather pretty."

Before, he might have wondered whether a having "rather pretty" home meant his townhouse was too fancy for someone of his class or not fine enough for someone of hers. Now he knew her better. Class disparity no longer mattered.

They had far more important differences to resolve.

"I didn't invite you here to show off my flat," he said without emotion.

Ironic, given that for weeks, it had been all he'd thought about. Dahlia sitting exactly where she was now. Belonging there. The two of them sharing meals, the marriage bed, their lives. He had imagined that with her present inside these walls, the house would finally feel like a home.

Instead, it felt like failure.

He took a seat a good distance across from her. "When did you start?"

"When I was in too deep not to," she responded. She hadn't asked for context or clarification for his question. They both knew why she was here. "I had less than forty-eight hours left to settle accounts, before the creditors removed us forcibly from the abbey. There wasn't enough money for both rent *and* food. Yet I had sixteen hungry children counting on me for their next crust of bread."

His voice was ice. "So you stole."

"So I stole," she agreed defiantly. "Someone had just ruined hundreds of pounds in donations that would have covered months of food and clothing. The charm I slipped into my reticule meant little to its owner. But it's worth would mean everything to my wards. That was the first object I stole. And the owner had it back within a fortnight."

"Because you pawned it."

"Because I sent a note telling him where to find it." She lifted her chin. "Feel how you like about my methods, but my intentions have never been to cause lasting harm to anyone. The opposite. He could more than afford the trifle it cost to repurchase his bauble, and I was able to buy cheese and fresh linen to sew replacement dresses for girls who had outgrown their only gown."

"Who did you get to make the transactions at the pawnbrokers?"

"Whoever I could find." She shrugged. "I never frequented the same one twice. And I made certain whoever I sent to make the exchange was as nameless and faceless as any other nobody off the streets. Someone who would be forgotten before he was even out the door."

Simon raised a brow. "How could you be sure he wouldn't run off with your money?"

"I couldn't. But, as you've duly noted, it was never *my* money. I felt that if I were ever robbed of something I myself had robbed, then it would be no more than I deserved." She met his eyes without blinking.

"And now?" he asked.

"Obviously I cannot continue to pilfer from the ton."

"You could *try*," he said in a tone that indicated what would happen if he caught her again.

"I promised you I wouldn't." She hunched her shoulders. "I'll find another way."

He frowned. "*Is* there another way?"

"I don't know," she answered miserably. "If I did, I would have tried it long ago. I have a partner now, which helps. I'm working on an event I hope will be far more successful than my past donation-raising attempts. But I still have creditors. Still have children who are often dressed as patchwork dolls because we haven't funds for proper wardrobes. Still have a larder whose empty shelves somehow have to fill twenty-four bellies."

"What will you do the next time you cannot afford your rent and the next meal?"

"I suppose I'll have to decide," she replied, her voice empty. "If I cannot provide for my wards, I will have to set them free."

Free. Like releasing a dove into a den of foxes. Simon's stomach churned.

He did not wish to think about what would happen if the boarding school closed doors. He already knew. They both knew.

The moment Dahlia failed to pay her creditors and the children were forced from the abbey, every one of those girls would be right back where she was before. Workhouses. Brothels. Surviving on the streets.

He could not accept such a horrid outcome for any of the girls. Molly, Beatrice, Louisa—every one of them had burrowed into his heart. They weren't faceless charity cases. They were like family.

Much like he'd imagined Dahlia would one day be.

He pushed to his feet.

She leapt to hers, her gaze hollow. "Is this interview over?"

"For now." He crossed to the sideboard and found a pencil to scribble an address onto the back of one of his calling cards. "Meet me at this address next week. I'll send you a time."

"What are you going to do?" she asked, alarm in her eyes.

He straightened his shoulders. "Change the future."

Chapter 34

Dahlia stared across the long rosewood table at Simon's solicitor. "*How* much money?"

"It's not enough to provide complete financial security," Mr. Gully cautioned her. "But it is enough to purchase the abbey outright."

Her head was still spinning. "You had an investment account of this size all along, and couldn't even be bothered to purchase so much as a carriage?"

"Actually, no," the solicitor answered gently. "A significant portion of the balance came from Mr. Spaulding's sale of his flat."

She slanted a shocked look toward Simon. He was incredible. "You sold your *house?* For my school?"

"It's not a pot of gold," he reminded her with a self-deprecating expression. "My father didn't leave me *that* much money. Once we make this purchase, every penny we own will be invested in a single piece of property.

The school will still need to rely on donations for all other expenses."

Faith glanced up from her copy of the documentation. "You refused to touch this money all these years because it came from the previous Marquess of Hawkridge?"

Simon's cheeks flushed. "That's right."

"I would do the same." Faith shivered. "I never did trust that family."

Dahlia ignored her best friend. She was too busy floating on air at the prospect of owning the abbey.

Simon had gifted the entire property to her and Faith. He wouldn't own so much as a broken tile. Then, as now, the boarding school would wholly belong to Dahlia and her best friend. A partnership split fifty-fifty.

"He's right." Faith pointed at a matrix of numbers on one of the documents. "There will be nothing left over for food or repairs, but at least there won't be creditors banging on the door."

It sounded lovely. It sounded marvelous. It sounded exactly like Simon.

"Marry me." She pushed to her feet and circled round to his side of the table. "The biggest mistake I ever made was walking away from you. If you're still willing to have me, there's no one I'd rather spend the rest of my life with."

He shook his head. "I think it's a bad idea."

The words sliced through her gut like a sword.

"I love you," she said, her voice cracking in its urgency. "I loved you when we were nothing more than a dashing Bow Street inspector waltzing with a headmistress in trousers. I can't help but keep on loving you for the rest of my life."

"I love you, too." His blue eyes locked on hers. "But you're not seeing the whole picture. You're elated because you and Miss Digby will now own the abbey grounds free and clear. If we marry, the law grants *me* full ownership of everything that was once your property. Miss Digby and I will be co-owners of the boarding school. You...will have nothing."

The law. Everything always came down to the law.

"You're wrong," she said, and reached for his hand. "I won't have nothing. I will have you. I'll have Faith. I'll have the school, no matter what it says on the paper. I trust you as much as I trust my own heart." She dropped down to one knee. "Won't you make me the happiest of women?"

Faith threw her documents across the table. "Hurry up and say yes, so that the rest of us can go vomit."

"*Yes.*" Simon pulled Dahlia up into his arms and gave a half-spin about the solicitor's office. "I would love to legally assume half-ownership of the St. Giles School for Girls from you against your desires."

She smacked him on the shoulder and lay her head to his chest in contentment.

Together, they would be unstoppable.

Epilogue

Dahlia clapped her hands. "Silence, please! The Circus Minimus is about to begin."

The school's shabby ballroom was stuffed fatter than a plum pudding. So many fashionable names had sent early donations to secure a reserved seat, they'd had to commission long wooden benches instead of fancy individual chairs just to shoehorn everyone into the same room.

On the dais was the night's three-person orchestra to accompany the performance: Mr. Heath Grenville at the pianoforte, Miss Bryony Grenville on the violin, and scandalous opera singer Lady Wainwright to provide soprano vocals.

Dahlia grinned at her siblings, then quickly took her place squished up against the back wall between her business partner and her husband.

Simon had managed to talk a judge and several magistrates into donating to the cause.

Faith looked like she might faint from so much proximity to the people who had spurned her in her youth—her face had particularly drained of color when Lord Hawkridge had entered the room—but Faith was made of sterner stuff. The last place she'd ever swoon was somewhere Hawkridge might accidentally catch her.

Dahlia slipped her hand into Simon's and gave it a quick squeeze. Under normal circumstances, a turnout like this might only be expected at an exclusive event as fêted as the Grenville family musicales.

This afternoon, however, all eyes were not on Dahlia's talented siblings, but rather on Dahlia's talented students. As the music began, so did the performance.

The delighted-to-be-shocked gasps as twenty-four schoolgirls filed into the ballroom wearing trousers and boys' shirts quickly gave way to stunned and utter silence as the girls began their routine.

Somersaults, pyramids, leaps from one shoulder to another. Her girls might not be ready to take on the Royal Amphitheater, but they were pretty bloody good. Their enthusiasm alone brought a smile to every face in the crowd as they tumbled over and under each other across the worn carpet.

When the music and the mayhem finally ended, the audience shot to its feet with thunderous applause.

Faith's idea to renovate a few of the rooms in order

to accept paying students just might work out after all. The donations from this performance alone would cover the other expenses for several months.

The first thing Dahlia planned to do with the money was to outfit a proper library, with at least one reading primer for every student. But the first thing she planned to do tonight...

She grinned at Simon and tilted her head toward the exit. "Care to spend the evening in our marital bed, Mr. Spaulding?"

"I intend to spend the rest of our lives in this abbey," he replied as he waltzed her toward the door.

Acknowledgments

Huge thanks go out to Morgan Edens and Erica Monroe for their advice and encouragement. You are the best! Any mistakes are my own.

Lastly, I want to thank the *Dukes of War* facebook group and my fabulous street team. Your enthusiasm makes the romance happen. I thought of you as I wrote this story.

Thank you so much!

Thank You for Reading

I hope you enjoyed this story!

Sign up at EricaRidley.com/club99
for members-only freebies
and special deals for 99 cents!

**Did you know there are more
books in this series?**

This romance is part of
the *Rogues to Riches*
regency-set historical series.

In order, the *Rogues to Riches* books are:

Lord of Chance
Lord of Pleasure
Lord of Night
Lord of Temptation
Lord of Secrets
Lord of Vice

In order, the *Dukes of War* books are:

The Viscount's Christmas Temptation
The Earl's Defiant Wallflower
The Captain's Bluestocking Mistress
The Major's Faux Fiancée
The Brigadier's Runaway Bride
The Pirate's Tempting Stowaway
The Duke's Accidental Wife

Join the *Dukes of War* Facebook group for giveaways
and exclusive content:
http://facebook.com/groups/DukesOfWar

**Other Romance Novels
by Erica Ridley:**

Let It Snow
Dark Surrender
Romancing the Rogue

About the Author

Erica Ridley is a *New York Times* and *USA Today* best-selling author of historical romance novels.

In the new *Rogues to Riches* historical romance series, Cinderella stories aren't just for princesses... Sigh-worthy Regency rogues sweep strong-willed young ladies into whirlwind rags-to-riches romance with rollicking adventure.

The popular *Dukes of War* series features roguish peers and dashing war heroes who return from battle only to be thrust into the splendor and madness of Regency England.

When not reading or writing romances, Erica can be found riding camels in Africa, zip-lining through rainforests in Central America, or getting hopelessly lost in the middle of Budapest.

For more information, visit www.EricaRidley.com.